The Orloj Of Prague

The Orloj Series Vol. 1

Erasmus Cromwell-Smith II

The Orloj of Prague
© Erasmus Cromwell-Smith II
© Erasmus Press

ISBN: 978-1-7330289-4-3
Library of Congress Number: 1-8463901031
Publisher: Erasmus Press
Editor: Elisa Arraiz Lucca
Proofreading: Charles Sibley, D. Suster, Tracy Ann-Wynter, Janet Bartos
Cover and Interior Design: Alfredo Sainz Blanco
www.erasmuscromwellsmith.com
Second edition
Printed in USA, 2022.

Books written by the author

In English,	En Español,

In English,

As Erasmus Cromwell-Smith II:
The Equilibrist series,
(Inspirational/Philosophical)
-The Happiness Triangle (Volume 1).
-Geniality (Volume 2).
-The Magic in Life (Volume 3).
-Poetry in Equilibrium (Volume 4).

(Young Adults)
-The Orloj of Prague (Volume 1).
-The Orloj of Venice (Volume 2).
-The Orloj of Paris (Volume 3).
-The Orloj of London (Volume 4).
-Poetry in Balance (Volume 5).

As Erasmus Cromwell-Smith

The South Beach Conversational Method
(Educational)
- Spanish
- German
- French
- Italian
- Portuguese

En Español,

Como Erasmus Cromwell-Smith II:
La serie El Equilibrista,
(Inspiracional/Filosófico)
-El triángulo de la felicidad (Volumen 1).
-Genialidad (Volumen 2).
-La magia de la vida (Volumen 3).
-Poesía en equilibrio (Volumen 4).

(Jóvenes Adultos)
-El Orloj de Praga (Volumen 1).
-El Orloj de Venecia (Volumen 2).
-El Orloj de Paris (Volumen 3).
-El Orloj de Londres (Volumen 4).
-Poesía en Balance (Volumen 5).

Como Erasmus Cromwell-Smith

El Método Conversacional South Beach
(Educacional)
- Inglés
- Alemán
- Francés
- Italiano
- Portugués

The Nicolas Tosh series, (Sci-fi)
- Algorithm-323 (Volume 1).
- Tosh (Volume 2).

As Nelson Hamel*
The Paradise Island series (Action/Thriller)
Dangerous Liaisons Miami Beach (Vol. 1)

The Rb Hackers series (Sci/fi)
The Rebel Hackers of Point Breeze (Vol.1)

(*) in collaboration with Charles Sibley.

All titles are or will be available in audio book.

Table of Contents

GLOSSARY:

"Characters"
- The Orloj.
- The Burly man (the street version of The Orloj).
- Thumbpee.
- Buggie.

"The Six Harlequins"
- Erasmus Jr. aka BLUNT; blue clothes Boston, Mass. USA.
- Sofia aka REDDISH; red clothes, Barcelona, Spain.
- Sanjiv aka FIREE; orange clothes; Mumbai, India.
- Winnie aka CHECKERED; black & white clothes; Pretoria, South Africa.
- Sang-Chang aka BREEZIE, yellow clothes, Shanghai, China.
- Carole aka GREENIE; green clothes, Beirut, Lebanon.

"The Six Statues"
- Cornelius Tetragor, statue of Humility; long white hair, ponytail, wears long robe.
- Lazarus Zeetrikus, statue of Pride; tall old man with a bent old hat.
- Lucrecia Van Egmond, statue of Generosity; long white threaded hair, pale skim aquiline nose, milky blue eyes, fine features, ankle long skirt, long sleeve shirt.
- Paulina Tetrikus, statue of Envy; short and hunched, short fuse, avoid looking in the eye, beautiful but angry face, short black hair, green eyes.
- Morpheus Rubicom, statue of Avarice; nervous, never sits still, puffy eyes, extremely skinny and tall, mat of wrangled curled hair, wears lose fitting, hanging clothes.
- Lettizia Dillettante, statue of Compassion; blond hair on a ponytail, statuesque, self-aware but humble. A Nordic beauty with a Mediterranean name.

"Other Characters"
- Erasmus Sr. (Blunt's father).
- Victoria (Blunt's mother).
- Zbynek Kraus, the antiquarian. Long white hair in a ponytail, Fumanchu mustache, wears electric blue robe and bent cone hat (both with stars and bolts).

"Clues Found"
- The tunnel's door lies underneath the old scribble, through the trickling river past your worst fears.
- Terror will be waiting in your path. Doubt and fear will ambush you unexpectedly only virtue will defeat them all.
- The six antiquarians, along with the virtues and flaws, will be present as you cross the tunnel.
- Only the complete knowledge of what you've learned along the way, will provide you the necessary wisdom to overcome the obstacles you are facing.
- Even though time will be pressuring and constrained. You'll have to ignore it completely. In order to succeed you'll need to act outside the shackles of life's clock ticking and ticking away.
- The dangers ahead of you as you move through the tunnel will test your good judgment and calmness under pressure, in the exercise of all you've learned.

"Dangers"
- The most imminent of all dangers will be among your peers, as your impulses to have fun and enjoy every moment could cause you to make serious errors that will get you expelled.
- Pay attention to the signs and symbols that will cross your path, they all have a great value and meaning for your journey of discovery. In particular be aware of the cosmic storms and northern lights, when they make themselves present it means that serious troubles lie ahead.

"Powers Earned"

- You can climb anything like spiders.

- You can walk through fire and ice.

- Your harlequin clothes will turn into street clothes when you are close or genuinely working with a statue. When your task is finished, you'll be back on your harlequin clothes. Be aware that if you have not completed your task and your street clothes are suddenly gone is a sign that imminent troubles lie ahead of you. It will also be a sign that you are not getting closer to a statue, rather farther away from it.

- You have the ability to know when anyone is lying.

- If your purpose is firm and clear, you'll be able to see through people and perceive who they really are.

- From now on you'll have the ability to create portals. This power will rotate among yourselves and only one of you will have it for each instance you decide to use it. Simply swipe your right hand in front of you and the blurry and translucent image of a wide door will appear in front of you. Only the six of you can walk through it. Simply step in and you will immediately emerge in a different part of the city, as long as you are all in agreement where do you want to go. If not, your destination will be at random.

- You guys will be able to be invisible when the situation arises. Be careful to use this power only when is justified. Otherwise, you may remain translucent for the rest of your life.

- You'll have the power to read what is on the mind of others as long as you don't show it to your target.

- Your powers will not work inside the tunnel or with The Orloj, Thumbpee, Buggic or any of the statues.

Note by the author,

My name is Erasmus Cromwell-Smith II. Following my father's footsteps, I am a scholar and a writer. In "The Equilibrist series" I narrated my father's life. In The first volume, "The Happiness Triangle", responding to the request of his former students, I revisited my father's memorable class of 2017 that took place at a prestigious Boston College. Thinking he was terminally ill, he narrated through poetry, his life's story commencing with his youth, and growing up in the Welsh town of Hay-on-Wye. He was surrounded by antique bookshops and eccentric antiquarian mentors that continuously tutored him up through his years at Oxford University. Subsequently, he fell in love during his post-graduate studies at Harvard with my mother, Victoria Emerson-Lloyd, the University's band baton twirler.

In the second volume, "Geniality", with additional material, I uncovered about my father's lectured classes, wrote about his equally masterful class of 2018, where after being miraculously cured by a state-of-the-art medical treatment, he took his class back in time —again utilizing the prism of poetry. He presented memorable tutoring sessions this time with New England Antiquarians and revisited the period when as a pair of youngsters, madly in love, he and my mom lived together at Harvard, until she inexplicably vanished.

In the third volume, "The Magic of Life" I covered his lessons of 2019, which turned out to be his last. With his students under the magical spell of poetry, he revisited one more time a series of existential revelations —my parents individually underwent— covering the period in time when they lived apart, up until the moment when they reunited and subsequently married. Then, barely a year later, my mother's eldest daughter and her husband perished in a road accident, which in turn led to my adoption by them as the orphan toddler of the deceased couple.

In "The Orloj Series" I narrate my own younger years. The first volume, "The Orloj of Prague" references my class of 2055, where copying my father's technique, I narrated for my students through the medium of poetry, a series of anecdotical experiences I had growing up, while being raised by my two middle aged adoptive parents. They were both former University Professors that devoted their hearts to my wellbeing and development. For this class in particular, I jumped into a series of overseas trips, where between the ages of twelve to sixteen years old, I had a number of "magical" life altering experiences visiting enigmatic and splendorous cities across Europe.

In summation, this and all the accounts of my life to follow, are meant to honor and celebrate my parents, Victoria Emerson-Lloyd, and Erasmus Cromwell-Smith Sr. Also, the unforgettable life we shared together, until their passing within months of one another, a bit more than a decade ago. Erasmus Cromwell-Smith II.

Written at T.D.O.K.
California's Central Valley 2056.

"Preface"

"The Central Valley Institute of Arts and Literature" encompasses 300 acres. Its numerous stainless steel and glass, five story buildings are all concentrated on the north side, situated on eighty acres of land that are slightly more elevated than the rest of the University's campus. The solar-panel powered structures are scattered all around the hill and they glow and shine in the distance like obelisks adjoining green areas; the faculty buildings look like a modern citadel, towering over everything.

My name is Erasmus Cromwell-Smith II. Immediately after graduation I was offered and accepted this post. So, I have taught literature and poetry at the institute since the tender age of twenty-one. That was fourteen years ago. During this time, I've become a tenured professor, following a family tradition. Being a fully accredited pedagogue, is exactly what my adoptive parents achieved during their entire lives spent at several universities in Boston. In addition to teaching being a pursuit, I've always loved doing, it is, what I was groomed to be since I was a child in the environment I was exposed to.

Like my father at my age, I am still single, but both in social behavior and outward appearance, that's where the similarities between the two of us end. I am 6' 3" tall, athletic, and eccentric. I dress in pastel colors, wear funny hats and preacher sandals. I carry my teaching materials in a sack with back-pack shoulder straps. My wardrobe makes me look like one of those strange businessmen from the Netherlands or Sweden. My peculiar choices in clothing are best described in a short verse one of my students posted a while ago, on my classroom's board:

I am notoriously chronically-tardy and informal about my curriculum. I can also be loud and passionate, but above all, I am regarded as an eccentric pedagogue. Analytic but emotional in circumstance, usually exacting and empathetic, but always inspiring. My beloved mother always cautioned me about her own trying love-life experience, and how it could affect and influence me, for good or bad.

"Would you be open to true love? Or would you run from it? Would your parent's scars from years apart drive you away from it, making you a reluctant lover? Or will our beautiful and lasting infatuation eventually drive you into your own version of it?" She pondered these questions as I grew up.

Fact is that my personal life is as colorful as my clothes. It is filled with multiple non-committal "friendship with benefits" relationships. My preference is for female athletes that can join me on my never-ending endurance sport crusades outdoors. But somehow my lack of long-term planning eventually intervenes, and almost inevitably, I get the boot. So, mother was right in a way, as what she sensed could be, is what in fact is actually happening. For no other reason, it seems that selfishness and self-preoccupation has me unwilling or perhaps not ready to go through the effort and pain that true love demands.

"Introduction"

(A World of Antique Books Everywhere)

And this is how my story begins...

Today as usual, it is already 8:05 AM, as Professor Cromwell-Smith II arrives at the faculty building on a Segway. Dismounting in a hurry, he walks briskly through the hallways for his 8:00 AM class.

On this, his first day of the 2055 academic year, he will have a student body attendance comprising 10500 participants, 500 of them in an auditorium, and the majority via a "live" web cast link from 200 various dominions nationwide.

The auditorium is filled with small virtual screens suspended in the air facing their anticipating viewers. Three remote-controlled cameras are pointing at the main stage covering every angle. A giant virtual video screen is suspended from the ceiling cutting right across the podium. It reveals continuous interactive viewing across the nation's dominions, of different participating classrooms.

The professor paces the stage with nervous energy, and as the students notice his presence, virtual screen after virtual screen vanishes. He does not utter a word 'til every one of them is gone.

"I want to welcome you all to our new academic year. Starting now, whether before, during or after the class, I don't want to see any of your personal communication devices — turned on—while inside the auditorium. This will be my only warning! Next time any of you transgresses this rule, you proceed at your own peril," he says with a grin on his face.

"This year, we are going to digress from the official curriculum," he announces fueling everyone's curiosity.

"With poetry as our guiding light, we will embark on a journey going back in time. Together we will revisit my life as I grew up," the professor continues with the inquisitive crowd. "As you'll see, my childhood years experiences were all centered around four journeys in magnificent citadels around the world. At each one of them I experienced magical and extraordinary adventures that impacted my development. Today and in a number of sessions that will follow, we will open up in the city of Prague."

The professor removes the sack from his shoulder and tosses it on the desk. He then rummages through it until he pulls out a couple of neat pastel-colored folders.

"Ready?" He asks.

The response he gets is a large number of nodding heads and an entire audience staring back at him with large wide eyes illustrating excitement and expectation.

He opens one of his neatly organized folders and starts to narrate in earnest.

Boston Mass. (2020s)

When my parents adopt me, they are both in their sixties. The good news is that the two of them are about to retire. Hence, I become the sole focus of their love and attention, the center of their universe. But there are some peculiar oddities about our family; for example, when her two older kids come to visit, naturally they refer to my mother, as Mom. So, they are supposed to be my siblings, right? Well, yes, they are, but they are also my aunt and uncle, as my mother was originally my maternal grandmother. It is really confusing for a five-year-old boy. On the other hand, I am growing up living with a pair of older folks, so my life experiences develop around their lifestyle. This consists of doing, what 'well-to-do' retired people do, which is travel the world quite often.

While we are traveling —both my parents being former teachers— I am home-schooled by them taking turns, hence, part of my childhood is spent circumnavigating he globe many times over; visiting the most boring things for a child, like old monuments, statutes, museums, historical sites, landmarks, buildings, operas, classical music concertos, just to name a few. We do this over and over. We do enjoy though, visiting Boston a few months a year, but seemingly just for a fortnight as we are soon, on the move again.

The better side of this is that I do get to visit every conceivable amusement park in the world. That is my reward for accompanying them on their never ending "history and general interest" tours. This all changes on my twelfth birthday, when unexpectedly, the old city of Prague becomes a door into a mystical and magical world, where I get to live and experience dreams and illusions, but this happens a bit later on.

My early childhood is comprised of a whirlwind filled with an abundance of love, attention and varnished and an avalanche of stimuli. My mother literally teaches me how to swim when I start to walk. In that same period, my father has me in no time riding a bike. As a consequence, soon after, I accompany them riding for hours at a time. My mother has me start sailing at an early age as well, teaching me everything she knows about the sea. Several times a week, when we are in town, my father takes me rowing on the Charles river, and fishing during weekends. To cap it all, I join both of them hiking during the summer through awesome mountain ranges and mountain skiing in the winter at places scattered around the world.

Many of the lasting and most memorable experiences of my childhood originate from my interest and aptitude for the world of books. To my delight, my parents provide reading material consisting of all the classic children books. This in turn makes me a voracious reader, creating a lifelong habit of exploring the vast world of books. Hence, omnipresent throughout, reading reigns supreme, additionally, when they have the time, they each love to read to me.

Alongside my mother I read most of Aesop's fables, the Brothers Grimm and Hans Christian Andersen's fairy tales and they all spark up a world of fantasy for me. My father and I read, Jules Verne: 20,000 Leagues Under the Sea, Journey to the Center of the Earth, and Around the World in 80 Days. H.G. Wells' The Time Machine, The Invisible Man and The War of the Worlds; Alexander Dumas' The Three Musketeer's and The Count of Montecristo; Mark Twain's Adventures of Huckleberry Finn, Tom Sawyer, and a Connecticut Yankee in King Arthur's Court, and Victor Hugo's Les Miserables; all of them opening doors for me of diverse cultures, places and lives of explorers, adventurers including exceptional sometimes mischievous characters.

My mother and I read The Arabian Nights: Aladdin, Alibaba, and Sinbad The Sailor; in addition to Peter Pan, Mary Poppins, Joan D'Arc, Moilier's The Misere and The Imposter. Additionally, I read, Uncle Tom's Cabin, The Pied Piper of Hamelin, The Nightingale, Dickens' Copperfield and Oliver Twist as well as Cervantes' Don Quixote. These readings help me further my ability to dream and expand my imagination so that I appreciate and value how rich, life and the human condition can be.

With my father accompanying me we read: King Arthur's Legend, Excalibur, Robin Hood, Ivanhoe, William Tell,

Ivanhoe, Daniel Boone, David Crockett, The Last of The Mohicans, The Alamo, The Brothers Karamazov, Blackbeard, Treasure Island, Robinson Crusoe, and Moby Dick.

Through them I visit worlds of courageous men confronting and overcoming seemingly insurmountable perils.

These and many other books that I have had the privilege to read and explore are like magic carpet rides that take me to awesome places that include exceptional and unforgettable characters that further enhance my imagination. The gallery of children classic books that my parents provide serves their intended purpose as a formative and exquisitely rich educational resource filled with joy, journeys, and endless life lessons. Introducing the art of reading at an early age and with such deliberate intensity, triggers in me innate talents and boundless creativity that not only expands without a narrow perspective, but in addition, opens the vastness of unlimited horizons. These amazing tales and stories cause me to grow up in constant awe and wonder about life and people, which in turn, permeates my character and persona, subsequently imbedding in me a set of virtues that include a perennially cheerful and grateful attitude for participating in the journey of life with its' fellow travelers.

I am certain that this strong proclivity of mine for the world of books, prompted what happened next, which totally changed the course of my life.

"Hay-on-Wye" Wales (2028)

A "Yankee Boy in Booktown" or "Yank" is how they refer to me here, though I rather see myself differently, more like a "Bostonian in a Welsh fishbowl."

Boston, my hometown, is far away across the Atlantic in New England. That's where I grew up, (when we were there). Until two years ago, just short of my tenth birthday, my parents decided, although it was mainly my father's idea, that my inclination for books would be best served, if the remainder of my formative years were spent surrounded with ancient writings available at my father's hometown.

"Junior, my hometown is famous throughout the world as a place where a large number of prestigious antique bookshops are concentrated, many of them well over 100 years old." My father explains this to me upon our arrival at the newly renovated and modernized family home. "Son, go ahead, roam and wander around town as I did when I was your age. I want you on your own to search and discover the treasures that surround you," he adds wearing a big broad smile on his face. "Once you settle on your preferences, I will occasionally accompany you to meet the antiquarians you befriend," he says with his parting words.

However, my father forgets a minor but crucial detail. I am on foreign soil. He wasn't when he grew up here! So, it has taken a bit more than a year for the locals, the school and me to get used to one another.

Four antiquarians end up on my favorites list, not only because they put up with the primitive ways of a youngster from "the former colonies", but also because of their willingness to share their shops treasures with me, especially those scribbles that they believe will serve me best in life.

My father told me that years ago, for a while, the town had a magic shop. He didn't like the place much as it dissipated any illusions, he had about magic being real. Years later, thanks to newly published masterful writings about the subject, a wizard and sorcerers craze hit the United Kingdom and then spread throughout the world.

Today, I walk across streets that are filled with the town's army of antique book shops. My destination is none other than my favorite place in Booktown. A store filled with books containing incantations, conjurers, charms, spells, witchcraft, enchanters, diviners and of course magicians, wizards, and sorcerers.

As I turn the corner the shop sign comes into view. It is only at a different place and time that the significance and the similarity of this particular antique bookstore will come back to me. But more of that later.

As always, either too afraid or too shy to enter, I glance through the shop window. Gigantic old books abound everywhere I peek. Through the dusty glass, I can see inside, a dark and cavernous place. This shop is simply the biggest I've ever seen. The titles all relate to my favorite topic: magic! I doubt that I'll ever be able to read much if any of these ancient books but that does not tamper my attraction to them. On tiny wooden stands that look too fragile for their voluminous size and weight, I focus on those on the display window that are closest to me. I can see them in great detail while I try to decipher their titles. Words from the world of magic abound. Suddenly, I freeze. The man, with piercing blue eyes and a mane of white hair all over his head and face, is staring intensely at me from the interior. I'm about to bolt when he gestures me to come in by bending his pointy finger. I am unable to move but what I really want to do is run away. Something I don't quite understand holds me back and yet, I don't dare to go in. The old man walks outside and invites me in.

The owner, antiquarian Winston Wildenkoss, is a rather peculiar fellow. Up close, his long bushy white beard makes him look rather enigmatic indeed. His penetrating blue eyes portray a mysterious and yet keen and observant mind, his electric blue puffy jacket is sprinkled with silver comets, planets, stardust; its color matches his equally oversized tam-o-shanter. The words he utters will stay with me for a long time.

"Young man. Patience is next what you keenly need to acquire. Soon, you'll learn more about it," he says pensively. "It'll happen closer to home. Then, you'll encounter it again in a location far away from here, but very similar in style to this place."

"Cornwall Peninsula" (2028)

My parents are intertwined. Mom's head leans over Dad's shoulder while they gaze in the distance at the ocean from the cliffs high above the coastline. I approach from behind, hold my father's free hand and join them in contemplation.

There is nothing I enjoy doing more with my parents, than the trips we take together from Wales to the Cornwall peninsula in England. The train ride from Hay-on-Wye to Tutro is cumbersome and intricate, but once there it quickly is erased from memory. Upon arrival we disembark along with our bikes, small backpacks and in an instant are on our way. We ride close to the coast, select a spot and park. That is our starting point for memorable walks, hikes, or a bit of both, that can last for hours.

We are all fond of the rough weather which this southwest corner of England provides in spades in the form of high winds, sea mists and an abundance of rain.

When we take a break at one of the plateaus that overlook the ocean, we sit right at the edge of the abyss over a red and white mantel and gulp down artisan sandwiches my mother has brought along. But the endless chats are what we treasure the most. It is during these moments of thorough spontaneous conversation, while enjoying the outdoors, that, especially my dad, transforms into an open book and window, sharing a world of profound wisdom and timeless life lessons.

"Erasmus, what is it with all this daily huffing, puffing, and steaming as if you are boiling inside?" My father asks.

My face darkens in a split second as the question brings back to the surface all of the uneasy recent memories that I'm holding inside.

"The kids at school keep picking on me," I blurt out.

"Why?" My father asks concerned.

"To them, I am either a yank or a nerd," I respond with the great relief that comes with revealing what is paining me.

"Dear, how long has this been going on?" Asks Victoria, my mom, with a hint of concern in her voice.

"Ever since we arrived," I reply nonchalantly.

My parents exchange a guilty glance at one another.

"Father, I constantly curse and by doing so I offend people," I state in angst raising my voice a tad to be heard in the wind-swept surroundings. "Also, when I'm not winning an argument, it becomes almost inevitable that an insult jumps out of my mouth."

My Dad seems to be lost in thought and not paying attention. I know better. After a pause that seems to go on forever, he turns and looks at me with complacent eyes.

"Son, I've had an earful from your mother and teacher about your recent conduct," he states surprising me. "I've been trying to figure out where your temper is coming from.

After giving it some thought, I've concluded that what is relevant is not whether your behavior is justifiable or genetically explainable but rather why you do it and what to do about it?" he says without blinking an eye.

"Today, I have brought along a book that I treasure. It is called The Magic in Life." He pulls an old blue book from his backpack.

My father indicates that we all sit down, and the effect of the breeze diminishes at once.

"Let me read something to you that exactly applies to your current predicament," he says as he opens to the right page and starts to read in earnest...

"The Weakness of Insulting Others"

We insult others when feeling less
than them or the situation we face.

Even though on the surface,
pejoratives appear to be directed at others,
what they reflect in reality,
is anger at ourselves,
out of feelings of inferiority,
perhaps frustrated at our incapacity
in a given moment
or reckoning with mediocrity.

Cursing others is also driven
by fear of being ousted
and our weaknesses noticed,
or our insecurities
about losing or not prevailing.

We put others down,
when artificially,
we try to feel better
or superior to them,
when in reality
we see them as better than us.

When we insult others
what we are really doing
in the final analysis,
is insulting ourselves.

When in the reflection of our conscience
in vain we try to believe,
there is a reflection of others
when in reality it is only us,
staring right back
and at no one else.

Hay-on-Wye (2028)

On my tenth birthday something that I cannot explain starts to change inside of me. My impulses are begging to take a hold of the cherubim and well-behaved boy that has been growing up. I become capricious, mischievous, and especially not respectful enough towards my parents.

"Son, it is apparent to me that you don't appreciate your life enough, you have an abundance of gifts that life has provided you," states my father while I stand by the door of his home studio, where he has ceremoniously summoned me.

I look at him in anticipation with eyes of resignation for another upcoming sermon, but I am in for a surprise.

"Come sit here with me, I want you to read something."

My father then proceeds to pull out from his library shelves what seems like a very old book and opens it to where it's marked.

"Read this my son."

"Patience"

Knowing how,
and knowing when to wait,
are the essence of patience.

Patience allows us
to slow things down,
as well as,
to control
abrupt-impulsive behavior.

Patience is a character quality
that requires
bountiful wisdom,
profound maturity,
absolute inner-peace,
immutable self-
control, and total
calmness.

Patience is a virtue
that provides us
with the best shot
at having "The Right Timing"

for anything
or anyone.

Patience is the best existential tool,
to "Cool Things Down,"
before we act
in the spur of the moment,
perhaps enabling us,
to realize mistakes or errors,
we may be about to incur.

Patience is a deliberate
"Lapse" in time
between Willingness and Action,
Rushing and Pausing,
Winning and Losing,
being Happy and Smiling,
regretting Sadly
and having Second Chances.

When we are besieged
by impatience,
it's sound to remember,
that in nature,
Morning will come,
Night will follow,
The Sun will rise
and at Day's End,
it'll reset all over again,
while moving alongside,
Nature's inexorable beat.

Everything happens in the Universe
for a reason
and at the right moment,
not a spec of time sooner,
not a fraction of a second later.

And there's always
a Cosmic or Divine reason
for time to behave in such way.

But, above all
Nature as its core
cannot be altered,
much less,
pushed, forced or sped-up.

Patience is, therefore,
an existential requirement,
as we chase and follow,
The Beat, Pace, Tics and Rhythm
of Life itself,
along with Nature, The Cosmos
and
The Universe as a whole.

"I like it very much, Dad. What a coincidence that the other day at the magic bookstore, the antiquarian informed me that I would soon be learning about patience."

"Well son, that wasn't a coincidence, it was a premonition of things to come."

"He also said that in a place far from here, I will encounter this."

Throughout the early years of my childhood, we visit many places around the world, but it is not until just shy of my teens that for the first time my parents take me to an antique bookstore, and that is where the story within the story really commences...

Chapter 1

"A Place of Countless Spires and Wizards"

Prague (2030)

By design or not, the first time my parents, take me to an antiquarian doesn't occur until I am twelve years old. It all happens on a summer trip to Europe where I discover what is to become one of my favorite cities in the entire world.

The narrow cobblestone streets in the city of Prague are framed by facades that seem to come straight out of fables or fairy tales from the medieval ages. Many of its buildings, mansions, bridges, estates, and city ornaments are both architectural pieces of art and engineering wonders. From the seven hills that dominate the city, the skyline seems impregnated with endless towers, all of them conspicuously hosting "pointing spires." Up close the facades are filled with enigmatic figures, the most notorious of them being, the intimidating gargoyles displaying the darker side of Prague. This citadel is at the same time a postcard of Gothic churches and Baroque palaces, both saturating it with an air of magic and mystery. Above all, the town as a whole is a timeless and splendorous monument, a living testimony to the craft and talent of its people who on one side are the regular folks that can be spotted every day on the city streets, in addition to those "other ones" that no one ever sees.

Today, I walk in between my parents, holding interlocking pinkies with each one of them. Wearing short pants, long socks, cute loafers, and perfectly groomed short hair, all of which I will eventually rebel against in the future; cheerfully and carefree we stroll the streets of Prague's Stare Mesto (The Old Town).

Earlier today, we walked over the magnificent and narrow Charles' Bridge spanning over the Vltava river, visited the mysterious Hradcany Castle (Prague's Castle) and the great safe-haven structure of St. Vitus Cathedral. Later on, we strolled through the fashionable pedestrian boulevard of Vaclaske Namesti (Wenceslas Square), and now we walk through Na Mustku street towards Staromestske Namesti (The Old Town Square).

At first sight everything looks simply spectacular. Right across the old town square, we can see The Gold-Kinsky Palace, The Tyn Church and The Statue of a National Martyr, Jan Hus. My dad explains that throughout the country, Hus is a revered figure, as simply because of his beliefs, he was burned alive on a stake in Konstanz, Germany in 1415.

"Vicky, do we still have time for a short walk to the Jewish Cemetery to pay our respects?" My father asks.

"Of course, dear, we still have a good half hour before the appointment at Nove Mesto (The New Town) with Kraus, the antiquarian. But that won't be a problem, since he is only a short walk away from here as well," my mother replies.

"Fine then, let's take a stroll over there, it will be a worthwhile visit."

'An antiquarian?' I chuckle as I realize that my parents are finally taking me to meet one.

We turn around in order to head in the direction of Prague's famous Old Jewish Cemetery. We cut across the big old town square of Staromestske Namesti. That's when I see for the first time from afar its magnetic blues and yellows. They immediately grab my attention. I pull both my parents fingers and drag them towards me. Thankfully neither resists.

"Dad, what is that?" I ask in excitement.

"The tower of the old city's townhall," he answers in delight acknowledging my curiosity.

"No, I mean the spheres on it," I correct him with a tone of intense curiosity in my voice.

"Ah, that is The Orloj," he answers matter of factly.

"The Orloj?" I ask incredulously, as just the name reinforces the enigmatic and puzzling feeling the city imposes on me.

"Son, The Orloj is Prague's world-famous astrological clock."

Little do I know that soon after, all my presages about the city will turn real and that the starting and central point of it all, will be the time instrument in front of us.

We are staring at the Lapis lazuli and pastel blues framing the yellows and gold colors of The Orloj. I feel an intense pull that I cannot explain. It also seems like I am being observed. For an instant it looks like the old watch is alive and glaring intensely at me. My inquisitiveness increases by the minute. I have to comprehend more about it. Am I delusional? A couple of kids my age, dressed in colorful outfits, are peeking outside, and scanning around the spherical clock. The Roman numbers that mark the hours, are in reality little doors that they've simply pushed open. I say nothing as they instantly disappear closing back the tiny clock doors.

Suddenly, a heavily accented voice bellows at our backs. I jump in surprise as the three of us turn our heads in a spontaneous reaction.

"Professor Cromwell-Smith?" There appears an old man with long white hair tied back in a ponytail and sporting a Fumanchu mustache,

"Yes?" Replies my father with a surprised tone.

"Zbynek Kraus at your service."

My father smiles and effusively shakes hands with the stranger.

"I know we are supposed to meet in a few minutes but as I was walking to my shop, I recognized you standing in front of the old clock," the eccentric Czech blurts out apologetically.

"Victoria, Junior. —which is how Dad called me at the time— "Mr. Kraus is a world famous and eminent antiquarian," my father states introducing him with ebullient enthusiasm.

"Well, I don't know about the eminent or famous epithets, but antiquarian definitely, yes. Nice to meet you Mrs. Cromwell and you too young man," he says delicately shaking hands with the two of us.

"Nice to meet you sir," my Mom and I respond in unison which makes us react in laughter at the unexpected chorus. This happens a moment before my exuberance gets the best of me.

"Mr. Kraus this clock is amazing. It is really awesome!" He squints while looking at me with a twinkle in his eyes.

"I guess curiosity runs deep in the Cromwell family," he says pensively before continuing.

"Well, there is much to be said about the ancient clock," the Czech antiquarian says distractedly pondering about it, as if he is sensing something in the future, something we still can't see...

"Mr. Kraus please tell me about THE ORLOJ!" I press him, emphasizing the name and interrupting his thoughts.

The mysterious name of the time machine affects everyone, as a piece that blends and fits perfectly into the moment.

"It would be a pleasure my acutely perceptive young explorer. First a bit of history. The Orloj is a medieval time machine, and it was put into operation in the year 1410, six centuries and twenty years ago. It tracks many different measures of time besides the European Central Time (ECT)," he emphasizes.

"Like what Mr. Kraus?" I ask inquisitively.

"Well, it tracks time in different ways. It measures Old Bohemian time where each day begins at sundown; it also measures Babylonian time where days are tracked only from sunrise to sunset; additionally, it shows Star time where time is tracked by the way stars move in relation to our planet's rotation; it also has a calendar dial that indicates the day, week, month, and year we are in. But the heart of the clock's mechanical operation is The Astrolabe, which keeps tabs of all the celestial bodies positions in the universe like the moon, the sun, and the stars," Mr. Kraus explains.

The eminent Czech antiquarian's dissertation offers direct and precise words. However, I am intrigued but not entirely satisfied. Mr. Kraus realizes it and seems puzzled. My parents are totally fascinated witnessing the exchange.

"What else, Sir?" I finally ask with intense eyes.

"What do you mean by what else? That is basically all of it," he affirms while squinting even more.

"No, you've only given me the obvious. Just history as it is written, there's got to be more to it, I can feel it, I can sense it. There's more, tell me about it Mr. Kraus," I plead with innocent eyes.

He finally smiles in surrender.

"There's much more to be said about the Orloj, but perhaps it would be better if we could continue this dialogue at my shop which is only a short walk away, shall we?" He invites us with a leading swing of the arm.

"It'll be a pleasure to oblige," my father responds excitedly.

That's how the three of us holding interlocking pinkies again, eagerly follow the eccentric antiquarian, through the narrow streets and alleyways of the old city, into what will turn out to be one of the most remarkable experiences of my childhood and perhaps my whole life.

As we walk behind and around the antiquarian, I start to hear strident voices and laughter. 'Am I going crazy?' The cobblestones street is filled with strangely looking and translucent characters that seem to be in every window and balcony, while some are even floating in the air against the old buildings walls.

"Here comes another calamity!" An old see-through man without teeth and dressed like a dirty ruthless pirate voices his prediction.

"Look at him holding pinkies with his parents. Is he a mama's or a papa's boy?" asks with loud laughter, a middle-aged woman dressed like the hostess of a medieval age tavern. "I'll bet you he is both," In a tone of scorn and sarcasm, answers an older woman dressed like a witch.

The sounds of awkward mockery keep increasing as we walk on but as I turn towards my parents, they are evidently not seeing, hearing, much less experiencing what I am going through. How is this possible?

Mr. Kraus on the other hand turns around, and for a brief moment, intensely squints at me. At that very moment I see a tiny almost imperceptible smile. 'Does he know what's going on?' I wonder and again decide to keep mum about it.

I suddenly jolt, feeling a disturbance. My parents instantly turn around to check on me. I am in a ridiculous pose as I try to look at my shoulder. I glance at them from the corner of my eye and realize that once again, they can't see what's happening as I stare at them with big wide eyes. I shrug my shoulders and they smile at me, but I don't!

A little man, not taller that my thumb, is seated on my shoulder. I don't have the foggiest idea how he got there. His skin is very peculiar. For some reason I can't focus on his image so I would describe him as a blurry milky yellow facsimile of a diminutive man.

"Erasmus, I'll accompany you during your quest," he says with his tiny voice.

'Quest, what quest?' I ask myself while a sense of premonition takes over, "who are you?" I whisper but my Mom overhears me.

"What is it dear?"

"Nothing Mom, just mumbling," I reply.

The little man just laughs while reclining on my shoulder his chin tucked in his hand. I frown at him with a questionable face.

"I am your conscience. I'll be with you all along the way to keep you honest. For now, I've got to go. Before I leave though, listen carefully to what I have to say. Don't be afraid of him, follow good old Mr. Kraus, he's a good man, follow him and he'll take you to The Orloj. I'll catch up with you later," he concludes, before jumping off and instantly vanishing.

"Is it my imagination?", I wonder all excited. The old city buildings and street seemingly are bursting with puzzling characters in every corner, roof, window, flight of stairs and even on my very own shoulders.

'Wizards, a city of magicians and sorcerers.' I think aloud in a soft voice, yet somehow, I sense that the same crowd is out there observing me, and they are, including Mr. Kraus, chuckling at my words.

A short while later, we turn from Zitna street into a small alleyway. Next Mr. Kraus unlocks his shop's main entrance wood and glass door and that's when we first see the surprising establishment's sign. The three of us stop right on our heels. It reads:

**"Zbynek Kraus, Antique Books Shop
for The Dark Arts and Occult Sciences
(est. 1993)**

As we step in, the sounds and ghostly characters of the street quickly fade, and I am left with doubts about whether everything has been an illusion. Are these just games that my imagination is playing on me? Or is it all real?

The doorbell signals our entrance into a different world. As we step inside, the peculiar smells of the establishment seize me. I can see on my parents faces that they appear as startled as me. For a moment, it seems as if they don't know what to do, but when they see my face full of wonder and my mouth open in awe, they both smile in complicity. The three of us promptly follow Mr. Kraus, who once in his shop, quickly disappears from view.

Right away, we feel a strong scent of incense mixed with perfume. It is so strong, that it prevails over the traditional smells of old leather, ancient paper, and dust.

There are also "little colored signs," posted everywhere.

"Incantations Available Upon Request."

"Conjure Here Anything You Wish For."

"We Can Impart Any Magic Spell
You Could Be in Need Of."

"Choose the Charm You May Desire,
it Most Certainly Resides Here."

"Witchcraft, Wizardry, Sorcery, Enchanting, Divining,
Benign or Black Magic, are all practiced at this shop."

As our eyes adjust to the dimly lit place, we realize the enormous size of the store in full display. There are rows and rows of dark wood shelves organized in a library type of style.

Mr. Kraus reemerges from the back wearing an outrageously eccentric electric blue cap and holding a cone flopped to the side hat, both of them in matching color. They are sprinkled with shiny, silver dust, stars, rays, and lightning bolts.

I am speechless with my mouth wide open, feeling absolutely mesmerized and hyper-excited as I recall the prediction made by the Hay-on-Wye antiquarian of magic books. My parents to the contrary, seem ready to burst into laughter, as once again my expression makes them not only refrain, but actually follow the flow. Mr. Kraus has fresh tea, lemonade and cookies waiting for us. Promptly, my father opens the reunion by following with the proper protocol.

"Mr. Kraus, we would like to express our eternal gratitude to you for spending your valuable time with us. My wife and

I requested this meeting well in advance, it is coinciding with a family trip to your lovely city. This occasion happens to be an important milestone for our family. This is the first time that young Erasmus has accompanied us on a visit to an antiquarian," states my father in full diplomatic throttle.

"It is a pleasure Professor Cromwell as your reputation precedes you."

"He loves books and has read most of the children classics," my mother proudly points out. "Erasmus Sr. grew up in Hay-on-Wye surrounded by antiquarians, so it runs in the family," adds my mother sounding a bit too eager to please.

Mr. Kraus gazes at me in delight and reflection. Finally, with a twinkle in his eye, sporting a big smile, he opens the door into his world of enchantments.

"Young man here is the perfect introduction targeting what you are about to experience," the old antiquarian cryptically says in a secretive tone as with gusto he begins to read from a yellowish scroll.

"An Upside-Down World"

The young girl protests. "Nothing works in here!"

Professes her mentor. "That is obvious and yet, not quite the way to think."

She asks impatiently. "How can I open any door?"

Quickly asserts her mentor. "By closing it."

She asks incredulously. "What about climbing a flight of stairs?"

Her mentor confirms, while showing infinite patience. "You can do that, but only by going down first."

The young woman asks in turmoil. "How do you do that, without being able to climb them first?"

He lectures with precision. "That's for you to figure out."

She declares in despair. "I can't. I'm paralyzed."

Her mentor confirms in resignation. "Yes, you are."

She declares while totally lost. "Don't know what to do."

Declares the young's girl's mentor steering her towards the wisdom of it all. "Actually, knowing you don't know, is a belief in itself."

She states trying to evade her predicament. "I am hungry."

Her mentor clarifies once more, with no logic at hand. "In here the only way to satisfy your hunger is by not eating."

She asks in contempt. "What kind of a place is this?"

Her mentor responds while staying on course. "One where nothing is what it seems."

The young woman babbles in disgust, but she is just trying desperately to put on a brave face. "I am sick and tired of your silly games."

Silence conveying obliviousness and obviousness ensues.

The young woman quibbles, rhetorically, all by herself. "Wait a minute, don't tell me that in order to take a shower, I simply don't, right?"

A relieved mentor states, recognizing the sudden progress of his mentee. "The wisdom of absurdity has begun to enlighten you, young apprentice."

The young woman vents. "I am glad you see it that way, because what I feel right now is contempt, sarcasm and utter frustration."

The mentor further drives his point across. "All you are doing is rejecting change."

Sarcastically the young woman asks. "What about this conversation, how come we are having it?"

Her "cynical deafness" is finally uncovered.

She says in realization. "Oh, I get it we are not having this conversation. This conversation is not happening."

The mentor affirms, correcting her once more. "No, to the contrary, we are indeed having one."

She claims realizing that she still doesn't have a clue. "What do you mean, I am totally confused."

The mentor asserts as the lesson inexorably takes hold of his mentee. "Our conversation exists, simply it is a non-conversation."

The young woman vents again without conviction. "This is all highly irritating."

Her mentor declares, sensing that he finally has his mentee's total attention. "What is unnerving you is that nothing in here is how it's supposed to be or what you are used to.

Change makes you so uncomfortable, that you resist or oppose it, not deliberately but viscerally."

The young woman disagrees, but only half-heartedly. "I think you got it all wrong, I simply am skeptical by nature."

Her mentor further explains as she nods her head in consent and agreement, for the first time. "No, that's a separate problem. Besides fear to change, you are rattled inside because you see the world in a certain way. You have a prescribed knowledge about how things work. To find out that such perception may be erroneous, completely unsettles and frustrates you. Your defense mechanisms and survival instincts are set in motion, your reaction is denial of that which discredits your vision of the truth and your belief systems."

She asks with a genuine desire to learn. "Why am I irritated then?"

"Erroneously, what you really feel, is inadequate in the situation you face and your interaction with people. That places you in a position of inferiority when handling the circumstances, you find yourself in. Thus, your reaction of anger or irritation is nothing but a protective shield, a defense mechanism. Your sarcasms and skepticism are only a reflection of how you feel about yourself. You respond by lashing out and criticizing or insulting others. Sadly, you're doing it out of feelings of inadequacy, inferiority, and frustration with yourself as you reject change."

As the antiquarian finishes reading, I am at a loss, and need to know how the scribble relates to the subject prompting my curiosity. Quickly, as if reading my mind, Mr. Kraus reveals it to me:

"Young man what you are about to experience, is a world where everything will seem upside down. Along the way there will be moments when you'll feel inadequate, even unable to contend with the situation. This will demand, on your part absolute flexibility to adapt and embrace change and overcome whatever stands before you, otherwise you will definitely fail." He explains all of this cryptically, but the usefulness of the lesson behind the poem still escapes me.

"Young Erasmus paraphrasing Machiavelli 'if you want to see people at their worst, bring them changes,' that'll be the biggest hurdle ahead of you," the antiquarian pontificates while allowing me to process his words as he challenges me one last time. "Tell me young man, are you certain that The Orloj is the only subject you want to explore?" Mr. Kraus asks, ignoring my puzzled look.

Despite my internal hesitation and growing fears, I look at him with mischievous eyes that communicate what they really want. As our stares connect with one another, the slight gesture from his eyebrows, almost imperceptible, gives him away. He realizes or at least perceives, that I am deadly serious.

My parents and I sense his eagerness as if he has been waiting for this moment a very long time. He lifts a small rug in a swooping movement of the hand and right in front of us, a humongous book is revealed. It's blue matches Mr. Kraus' own clothes. Its wizardry cover appears to be of the same fabric and glittering ornaments as well. With wide open eyes and an even bigger smile he opens it exactly where he intends to start reading in earnest.

"Staromestske Namesti"

"The old townhall tower looms large over the historical Staromestske Namesti (The Old Town Square). Its astronomical clock has been a witness to the topsy turvy life and progress of the Gothic city. Across from the tower lies the statue and memorial of the Czech national hero and reformist Jan Hus, erected on the square after he was burned tied to a stake in Konstanz, Germany in 1415. Then, on the old town hall tower itself there are six statues. Three representing human virtues, namely, compassion, generosity, and humility. Three representing human flaws, namely, pride, envy, and avarice. But the heart of the tower is "The Orloj" with its beautiful blues, yellows and golds, its huge dials, and its timeless hands. But nothing is what it seems to be on the vast pedestrian square. The Legend goes that ever since twenty-seven insurgents, including Czech noble men (three lords and seven knights) and Prague commoners (17 businessman called Burghers), were unjustly executed on Staromestske Namesti (The Old Town Square) in 1620, for rebelling against the King, Ferdinand II of Habsburg, strange things started to happen at the square and with The Orloj. First are the statues, and even though no one has ever witnessed it, the belief is that at odd hours and under peculiar circumstances, all of the statues come to life. Then there is The Orloj itself with its astrolabe, which is believed to be an entrance into a secret world. It is also rumored that The Orloj hands transform to humans and join the statues on the square. Finally, there is this ageless fable about a fraternity of rowdy and immature "wizard apprentices" dressed as harlequins that pass in and out of the ancient exacting machine during the wee hours of the evening."

Mr. Kraus stops reading while squinting with intensity, eyes riveted in my direction, his lips tightly closed. I shiver while holding my parent's arms, but my face is dead set eager to hear it all. That's how I return the stare, I want more, bring it on is my subliminal message.

"Young man, Professor, Mrs. Cromwell, for most mortals this is where the story ends. What happens next, depends entirely on whether our inquisitive boy's imagination can take him into the world of the young wizard apprentices. Only the very few chosen ones that fall under The Orloj's spell, gain access to it," he adds while in a trance. "I've sensed from the very first moment how your keen interest and curiosity turned into fascination. Soon after, as an outcome of your receptivity, you inadvertently and unwittingly fell into this world."

I can't quite follow the antiquarian's words. We all look at him puzzled. Unexpectedly, dizziness engulfs me, and I feel as if I am about to faint.

He enigmatically softly utters, "go ahead push the door."

My parents and the antiquarian are only a blur as their images quickly fade. In the distance I can still hear Mr. Kraus' voice. He adds but still making no sense to me, "young Erasmus, you now should be inside The Orloj."

…but that's when, in a void of time and space, magic happens…

Chapter 2

"The Orloj"

I find myself alone standing on a set of suspended narrow steps. I am surrounded by the wooden gears and mechanisms of a giant ticking clock. Its sound so strong that it deafens me. In front of me there are a couple of lit blue circles, one on top of the other. I stand behind them. I have no idea how I've arrived here. Without thinking, I do exactly what the wizard antiquarian just ordered.

At exactly 3 AM, based on The Orloj's Astrolabe's sphere, I slightly push forward a small door behind the three o'clock slot and everything is frozen in time at the old square. The startled 'burlesque' figures turn around in the direction of the ancient clock; after all, it's not all that common to welcome guests into their world.

Sticking my neck out, I peek outside the sphere, and what I discover totally blindsides me. Staromestske Namesti (The Old Town Square) is filled with colorful harlequins —as in vivacious youthful court jesters— engaged in all sorts of acrobatic mancuvers. As spectators, I see six moving statues observing it all, as well as what appear to be a pair of clock's hands, one taller that the other, engaged in a lively conversation with one another. The stone floor is illuminated with beams of light projecting lively pastel colors, portraying an utterly surreal scene.

As my eyes adjust to the intense lights, I realize that the figures are looking at me. Even more shocking is the realization that all the harlequins are children of the same age as me. I quickly count five of them, all leaning on one another, some standing, some kneeling, like a group of old pals.
I push the door within the sphere further out, and see a small scaffold lying outside, leaning against The Orloj. Nevertheless, though still shell-shocked, I continue to move forward as if driven by a ghostly force. I step out of the ancient clock onto the feeble platform, and face the small crowd, now gathered ten feet beneath me.

'Where are my parents and Mr. Kraus? How could it be totally dark when it's only midday?' I wonder aloud with overwhelming angst.

"When your highness is ready, please dispense us the honor of walking down the scaffold," a sarcastic and impossibly young, yellowish harlequin of Asian origin instructs me. It is hard for me to distinguish if it is a boy or a girl.

Haranguing me in a more direct fashion, an orange harlequin boy, with deeply tanned skin and intense eyes delivers the words, "what are you waiting for?"

Now I am in for another big surprise. It happens when I extend my arm, grab the rail, and descend down the steps. My clothes are now like theirs. I am dressed exactly like them, I am a harlequin, a white and blue mime, and a Jester!

No sooner do I step on the ancient stone grounds of the square than my fellow harlequins pile on me. At that moment I feel like a grown up twelve-year-old at a playground with unruly out of control five-year-old children.

A green-eyed harlequin girl, seemingly from the middle east, dressed in matching color says, "welcome Erasmus, we have been waiting for you to arrive so that we can complete our trainees' squad."

Trepidant, I ask "trainees squad for what?"

A red haired freckled harlequin girl with matching clothes, seeking restraint from the others points out, "c'mon guys take it easy with our new member, weren't you equally clueless when you landed here?"

"We all are, including you, aspiring to become wizard apprentices," she says.

I complain aloud. "But I didn't ask to become one."

A checkered harlequin girl with beautiful ebony skin responds. "Yes, you did, we all saw the images of you on the sphere of The Orloj, and the way you cajoled Kraus the antiquarian was relentless."

I start to reject this, but she rebukes me at once.

She says decisively. "No doubts, you invoked The Orloj and here you are, your wish has been granted."

I ask still not getting it, "what is all of this? Just moments ago, I was with my parents at Mr. Kraus' antique books shop, it was the middle of the day!"

She wisely replies, "well you are here now, so you may as well make the best of it!"

I suddenly recall Mr. Kraus' words and they begin to sink in, "...it will demand absolute flexibility to adapt and embrace change, otherwise you will definitely fail..."

While gazing intensely at each other, we all fall silent for a moment. My eyes continue to project a large inquisitive sign, but I do not want to say anything that will ridicule myself even more. The red-haired harlequin girl deciphers me with pinpoint accuracy.

She asks, "what do you want to know?"

I continue, "what is this place?"

"We are at present, in an alternate reality."

Before jumping the gun again, and although still clueless, I remain silent, intent on learning what this is all about.

"At this moment, Mr. Kraus and your parents are experiencing time elapsing at a different pace than yours. When you return to them after a little less than one day's time, only a few minutes will have gone by for them, so your absence will hardly be noticed. They will though comprehend, a vague and foggy idea about where you've been and what you've been doing so, you'll have very little to explain to any of them."

The angst starts to subside replaced by a feeling of excitement and wonder. The red-haired harlequin adds that, "the Prague you are in, is a city populated by wizards. In fact, in the world of the dark arts and the occult, Prague is known to be our planet's Wizard center. It is heavily comprised of magicians, sorcerers, enchanters, conjurers, diviners from all sorts of life, some pursuing good others simply chasing evil."

An unexpectedly thunderous voice abruptly deafens everyone and drowns out all sound.

"The Orloj of Prague"

"In order to get started, young Erasmus, the other five harlequins and I have been waiting for you," announces The Orloj, while everyone in the square turns their heads towards the mammoth clock.

The old clock continues as everyone listens. "Your mission is to find the tunnel that runs underneath the Vltava river and into Hradcany Castle (Prague's Castle). In it lie your credentials for becoming a true certified wizard apprentice. Six clues are to be found in no particular order, scattered around town in the most unexpected places, when discovered, will enable you to make entrance into the castle. Each clue will be earned and revealed after you have demonstrated mastery of any of the exceptional human virtues; compassion, generosity, humility and also that you've learned, the hard way how to endure the set of abhorrent human flaws; pride, envy, and avarice. The six statues that on a daily basis adorn this tower in the normal mundane reality, in our alternate world can be found residing somewhere in the streets of Prague. Each of them represents one of the character virtues of life that you are trying to master (the statues of virtues) as well as one the character flaws you need to avoid (the statues of flaws). My statues are hard to find or detect, as they morph according to circumstances or in reaction to who is addressing them. Their preferred occupation is that of antiquarians, but they could morph into beggars, street performers, artists or almost anyone you may encounter in the streets of Prague. Three of them are always truthful and humble but exacting and extremely demanding. The other three are misguidedly funny, easygoing on the surface and will sometimes disguise themselves as statues of virtue, but they are always very deceitful, onerous, dangerous, and damaging. You'll need to uncover them all in order to find the path to Hradcany. Note that for you, this alternate world will only exist over the next twenty-four hours, after which you'll resume your regular life. Take advantage of every minute you are in it, because if you earn the right to revisit it'll be available only once a year. This will take place across four different European locations on the anniversaries of the deaths of the martyrs of this square. Always remember that around you nothing is what it seems to be. The six statues, and others, will steer you either closer or further away from the clues you are searching for, nevertheless, in order to progress and advance, you'll have to face each one of them and master the life lessons they represent. My two children "the two hands" will be with you all the way and will keep me informed. Call upon them anytime you wish. Every time you are in possession of a couple of new clues, you will have earned the right to come over and ask me for further guidance, advice, and wisdom."

The Orloj bellows and a heavy and powerful laughter emotes, "I seldom move around. This tower residence is quite comfortable and cozy for me. To leave, though my age and weight also play a role, is never an issue for me. When the situation requires it, I make myself present and inevitably heads roll. Youngsters, believe me you don't want me around under any circumstances. Young Erasmus, you are amongst a very small group of youngsters that have managed to make it all the way to me. I want to caution you that being here, even though, it is a privilege, so far it means nothing per se, because like your fellow aspiring wizard apprentices, you are starting from zero and this will not be an easy feat. There will be danger at every turn and throughout your path, your courage, persistence, and imagination will be tested. Temptation will seduce you with open arms only to entrap you to cause failure. Furthermore perhaps, the most imminent of all dangers will arise from amongst your peers, as your impulse for having fun and enjoying the moment will cause you to make serious mistakes that will get you expelled. Enjoy every minute of your quest to gain wizardry, have fun, but set boundaries that clearly delineate what your limits are, and how much entertainment is enough. Always keep in mind that this city is best deciphered from above. Let's address the issue of your powers. Erasmus, every time you step into this alternate world, you'll be in possession of several magical powers. It'll be up to you to discover what they are, and how to make good use of them. These powers will increase in number as you master each one of life's virtues and flaws. As you discover more of the clues, your powers will diminish every time you use them inappropriately. Every time you return to this world, you'll have the same powers you had when you left. Pay attention to the signs and symbols that will cross your path. They will have great value and meaning in your journey of discovery. In particular be aware of the cosmic storms and the northern lights showing up across the night sky, when they make themselves present it means that serious troubles lie ahead. Finally, your harlequins' costumes, will disappear when you are genuinely at work searching for the three virtues or the three flaws. Your harlequin clothes and appearance are designed so everyone in the city will notice you. These characters will stay out of your way as they all know that you are the new crop of aspiring wizard apprentices."

The Orloj announces before he goes into hibernation again, "this doesn't mean that you are exonerated from following the law. If you break it, you'll suffer the consequences like everyone else. One more thing, be aware of the gargoyles, malefic statues that inhabit and roam Prague's rooftops. Some are as they appear, menacing, mean spirited creatures. Others have the shape of small dragons or even the devil himself. They'll be constantly shadowing you, jumping from rooftop to rooftop, ready to strike whenever they sense weakness in any of you. It'll be hard for you to identify any of them, as they'll shape-shift, morphing and staging different approaches, trying to tempt or deceive you into doing the wrong thing, by making a mistake, an error in judgment or even forcing you to quit the quest. Even though they cannot harm you, their sole purpose is to get all of you to fail. Your twenty-four hours commence right now!"

"The Quest Begins"

The place suddenly feels empty without the imposing personality, thunderous voice, and intense energy of the living clock, but as the sounds of the city night make themselves present, they immediately capture our attention. We hear little bells ringing intermittently somewhere in the vicinity, swooshes of wind whistling, the buzz of tiny wings batting furiously coming and going, a powerful scent of incense is all around, noisy laughter in tandem echo and reverberate throughout the square followed by other sounds. From the opposite direction we see and hear the strident voice of an old man with a longish white beard, wearing a long robe babbling an unintelligible dialect, talking to a group of similarly dressed senior citizens. The old man speaks in a sarcastic tone as if his teeth were tightly clenched together. Suddenly, we see a group of young girls arguing while walking into the square. They are dressed in clothes originating during the Victorian era. The sparks emanating out of them are what unexpectantly blind side us. Intense and bright yellows in the form of tiny lightning bolts seem to jump out of their heads and fingers as they speak impossibly loud to one another. That's when the first flying creature encircles us. It wears an incredibly tall top hat bent on one side, a duck tail suit of opaque colors, in sharp contrast with a bright striped vest, its face is endlessly elongated, its nose humongous, long and its bright orange though sparse beard and mustache border on the ridiculous. Floating right in front of us, in a standing position it observes each one of us with keen and highly skeptical eyes.

It utters in a loud voice, "another pack of novices," then without a moment's hesitation rapidly flies away.

In the middle of the square, shaken and stirred, we circle, and size up one another. Although no one has said it yet, the fact is that none of us knows what's going on or what to do next.

In the spur of the moment, I blurt out, "wicked jiminy crickets!" as the others nod while wearing totally spooked faces. Trying to break the ice I ask, "when did you guys get here?"

The freckled face girl with red hair announces, "we all got here within an hour of your arrival. We are all first timers, and you were the last to enter and join us. We all seem to have in common an obsession with The Orloj. That's precisely what has brought all of us here."

"By the way, my name is Erasmus but while we are here you can call me Blunt. I am from Boston, a city in the USA."

"I am Sofia and go by Reddish. I am from Barcelona, Spain."

"Sanjiv, please call me Firee. I am from Mumbai, India."

"My name is Sang-Chang. In here, I'll be Breezie. I am from Shanghai, China."

"At home they call me Winnie but in here, please call me Checkered. I come from Pretoria, South Africa."

"I'm Carole, but please call me Greenie if you don't mind. I originate from Beirut, Lebanon."

"Has anyone noticed that we are the same number of participants as there are statues?" I ask but the blank looks of the other five scream total ignorance, so no reply is expected. I point to the tower's clock, "Also the statues and the hands of the clock are gone."

Firee blurts with a puzzled look on his face. "Back at the square, they already were gone shortly after you arrived."

"That's precisely what The Orloj said, that in this alternate world they morph into people, and we have to locate them." Then I suggest in reply, "why don't we get moving?"

Reddish puzzlingly asks, "what are we supposed to do now?"

Breezie responds, "what about getting to the rooftops?"

Checkered adds, "yeah, the old clock said that the city can be seen better from above."

"Well, right here on the square we have a small palace and a cathedral so let's check which roof is easier to reach," I conclude taking the lead.

We stroll tentatively in the direction of the two tall buildings. Getting acquainted with my peers is unsettling in the beginning. After all, this is my first experience with children my age from other countries. I take stock while gazing furtively at them. Breezie is a smart acrobatic boy from China, Greenie is a beautiful and emotional girl from Lebanon, Reddish a passionate and opinionated girl from Spain, Checkered, a timid but profoundly intelligent girl from South-Africa and Firee is a vivacious and endlessly curious boy from India.

"Don't you have the feeling that we are being watched?" A spooked Greenie asks, her voice a whisper.

Stealthily, the gargoyles move through the shadows of the night. Whether attached to ledges, balconies, vertically or horizontally. They detach from their bases, scatter about and are constantly watching and tracking us, the young harlequins who are seeking to become wizard apprentices. Although they easily conceal their menacing forms, their eyes give them away. Twosomes of intense evil light, pairs of dark red, green or yellow irises seemingly bore into their prey without an iota of goodness secreting from them.

No one answers as we all feel the same trepidation and fear. The beautiful architecture now seems menacing. Sure enough, as we pan through the skyline and the countless darkened streets and alleyways, we see them, but only when we move our heads and shift our eyesight rapidly sideways. There they are seemingly countless imposing pairs of eyes watching over us in this city of wizards from within the darkness of night.

We all stop and look at each other in disbelief realizing that they all are viewing us. Once again one of us tries to deflect the moment and alter the intense emotions rising up that are affecting our thoughts.

"Blunt, I think The Orloj may just be a Troll without any good intentions at all," Firee remarks.

As I start walking for the first time, I notice the moving shadows.

"Hey guys look up," I say pointing at the rooftop of a small building on the perimeter of the square.

Taking a few steps at a time, we see what were still shadows now moving in a procession across the roof of the cathedral. Then the first in line presses his extended arms against his sides and taking a little jump, simply drops. Everyone else when it's their turn follows suit.

"What are they doing?" Reddish asks.

I reply, "don't you think, we might as well try to find out?"

"You are all able to climb on anything imitating spiders. So, use your powers," surprisingly my thumbnail conscience whispers from my shoulder, when I turn my head towards him with a puzzled face, he is again gone!

Then, feeling totally frustrated as I lean over a streetlamp, my body suit adheres to the post. When I try to untangle myself, the same thing happens to my hand and right foot. Intuitively, I simply climb, unclimb and untangle myself by just thinking about it. Next, one by one, all the other harlequins try the same feat against a building wall, and soon they realize that the same ability that has been bestowed on all of us. Soon we scale up through the facade of the cathedral. In the meantime, the sounds of the wicked city continue reverberating into our hyper-sensitive ears. From the rooftop of the cathedral under a full moon we can see the entire city, but the shadows are nowhere to be seen. At first, we only hear the grunts then we see them again, right there in the middle of the cathedral's sharply inclined roof, the same group of long robed men with massive white beards, we saw earlier at Staromestske Namesti (The Old Town Square). They again are having an animated discussion, but upon seeing us, they halt and hastily leave. We follow, and they move even faster until they reach the rooftop's ledge. They turn around once more, look at each other with puzzled faces, in resignation shrug their shoulders and simply fly away, except for the one who stays just for a fraction of a second longer.

As he prepares to lift off, I react without thinking, "wait, wait, don't leave yet." I shout while trying to catch my breath as I hurriedly approach him. "Can I ask you something?"

The old man turns around glaring at me with intense eyes. His face wears an expression of disdain and does not seem very comfortable with me interrupting whatever ritual he is performing.

I plead, "Sir, perhaps you can help us," recognizing him as the leader of the group at the square that earlier was arguing with the others. I comprehend that this is routine behavior for these folks.

There is no response from the old man as he seems to hesitate, his eyes darting in both directions. Instantly, he shrugs his shoulders and with a sweeping hand gesture invites us to follow him up to the roof. We all follow him taking bouncy steps on the sharply inclined roof. When he reaches the pointy tower, he touches the yellowish brick's surface, and an old wooden door instantaneously appears. On the mantel at the top there is a store sign. As we hike up the roof incline, we realize that we are all wearing our normal street clothes.

'Your harlequin personas will disappear when you are genuinely working on any of the six statues, the three virtues or three flaws.' I recall The Orloj's words as I focus on the oddly located store sign. It reads:

**"Cornelius Tetragor,
Antique Books for The Spirit and The Soul"
(est. long, long time ago)**

We follow him and enter into a tight roundish space. The books are on display by the thousands as they're crawling up the cylindrical walls of the tower, filling bookshelves that rise several stories in height. A couple of wooden ladders stick out due to how narrow and impossibly long they are.

Reddish asks with pompous diction, "you are Mr. Tetragor, shall we presume."

He responds with an almost imperceptible nod.

"We are searching for the six statues," I blurt.

"Have a seat you all," he commands, directing us to six tiny stools situated in the center of the roundish store.

"I'm indeed, Cornelius Tetragor and have nothing to hide. I am also one of the statues, and in fact, hold one of the clues. If you demonstrate that you have learned the virtue or flaw I represent, then you'll walk out of here, figuratively speaking, with one of the clues. However, if you don't succeed, you will have to return again, but only after you are in possession of the remaining five clues."

Mr. Tetragor without saying a word, climbs along one of the ladders, continuing until he is only a small dot high above his peculiar store. He then descends at full speed with his hugging legs and arms sliding down the ladder's sides. We are all delighted with the stunt, but it is a short-lived event as Mr. Tetragor is wearing a solemn face when he lands back at ground level.

"This is a tale that will serve us well in the lesson we have at hand. Let me read it to you," he offers as he moves, adjusting an old and dusty brass lamp while sitting on a humungous ragged sofa. In slow motion he observes each one of us with his head slightly tilted forward and his reading glasses resting at the tip of his nose. Apparently satisfied, I see him wearing a faint almost imperceptible smile as in earnest he starts reading.

"The Young Boy and The Lion"

Along the Zambezi river he walks,
the young boy from Zimbabwe.
The sudden roar freezes him.
Right on his back a mighty lion seizes his prey,
A second roar follows,
it is quieter and deliberate
as if in slow motion,
Kunte senses the lion as tension builds up,
'He is ready to attack,' the young boy reasons.
Kunte turns around enough to see the fiery look

on the king of the jungle's eyes.

It is precisely at that moment
when the Words of Wisdom of Yeti,
his mentor and the tribe's conjurer,
come to use.

"Kunte, the key to bond with the wild beast
is to control your fear and to show humility."

While staring at the lion,
the young boy slowly bows his head.
The effect is immediate
as the lion seems to relax
and does not move forward.

Then to Kunte's great surprise,
without taking his eyes off the young boy,
the magnificent beast lowers himself
and lays down on the ground.

Having heard both roars,
Yeti fears the worst,
so, he runs desperately through the bush,
in search of his beloved mentee.

As he sees the river come closer,
there they are,
staring at each other,
the young boy, and the lion.

The wild animal immediately senses Yeti

and turns his head towards him.
The frantic fear in the eyes of the conjurer
crosses the calm eyes of the beast.
The lion tenses and stands up.
A frightening roar follows.
Yeti stops right in his tracks
and prepares for the worst
as he is in the crosshairs of the wild animal.

That's when an amazing and magical moment happens...
The young boy takes a step forward
and the lion immediately turns around towards him.
The body language of the beast announces a roar,
the head and the jaw make the movements,
but there is no sound coming out of the lion.

With his head still bowed
and an extended arm reaching out,
Kunte continues to approach step by step
the mighty king of the jungle.

Yeti, the old conjurer, is overcome by emotion
and a couple of tears slide down his cheeks
as he sees Kunte, the young boy,
first pat, then hug with his two arms
and finally kiss, the beautiful lion.

Completing the presentation and to stimulate discussion
Cornelius Tetragor asks, "Young apprentices, what did Kunte
display to gain the lion's acceptance and ultimately his heart?"
"He wasn't afraid," affirms Reddish.
"He was confident," says Firee.

"He acted with meekness," reasons Checkered.

"He was humble," states Greenie.

"He was unpretentious," declares Breezie.

"He acted with modesty," I affirm.

"All of your perceptions and understanding are true, as he displayed fearless courage, absolute self-confidence, and profound humility. There is however, another crucial and timeless lesson to learn from this fable. The actual underlying enabler of his behavior and what really captivated the lion, was Kunte's demonstration of unfettered and genuine respect. Youngsters, it is self-evident that humility is driven by courage and self-confidence; but our respect for others precedes this, as it is the genesis out of which humbleness is born. In its absence humility doesn't resonate with those to whom we attribute modesty," insightfully concludes Cornelius Tetragor.

We all speechless sit around the old man with the long robe and a massive white beard. Finally, we see a faint smile that seems to indicate his satisfaction. Then, in one movement he sweeps his hand in the air, and instantly we find ourselves back in the inclined roof of the cathedral. Other than the big envelope I am holding in my hand, there is no trace of him.

"Humility," is what it reads.

We all jump, cheer, and hug each other in celebration of our first clue.

No sooner do we read aloud the words on the cover of the envelope, than my conscience is again sitting on my shoulder!

"You should not open it now," the tiny, d i m i n u t i v e man, whom from then on, we call Thumbpee, advises me.

"Why?" I ask.

"Because —outing the clues— is best when it occurs in pairs and includes their opposite which in this case is pride."

"What about speaking with The Orloj for advice?" Asks Greenie.

"It's much better when you have two clues since then he'll be able to help you even more," Thumbpee responds.

"What is our new power?" Breezie asks.

"From now on, you will be able to successfully walk-through fire and ice. You better get going since the night is short and the clock is ticking," Thumbpee instructs us and as he usually does vanishes instantly.

"Ok, let's go."

As I announce this and to everyone's surprise, we are all back in our harlequin tights.

Moving deftly, we reach the two rooftop spires. A few buildings away, we again can see the shadows line up as they continue to jump down with a little hump.

"Blunt, some of the shadows are flying, watch!" says an exhilarated Greenie.

"Many others also are jumping but instead differently targeting building to building. Look! Incredibly they're using the spires as catapults to spring from rooftop to rooftop," observes Firee.

We all see a shadow leaning on a spire pushing it with her back. Next, the snap of the bent spire acts like spring sending the shadow flying onto the next rooftop. Observing the city skyline, in the same manner we find hundreds of shadows springing from rooftop to rooftop. Tentatively at first, I push a spire with my hand to get a feel for the action. Kids being kids, we all recognize and chase fun at all times. Soon, I'm facing the closest rooftop and once more I push the spire but now with my back and disregarding the consequences I let go...!

Precipitously, I am propelled into the sky with enormous force. I shout enthralled and smile from pleasure until I lose momentum and even though I am still moving forward, the fall is precipitous, I'm gaining —gravity induced speed— by the second. I yell but now in panic as the targeted rooftop approaches at full speed. I brace for impact but within fractions of an inch just before I smash against the rooftop, the speed is gone, and I land softly by simply planting my feet on the surface.

"Yeah!" I scream at the top of my lungs while I wave at the others to follow me.

It takes just a few minutes for we six to become —rooftop jumping— harlequins. Crazy ones though, as Reddish misses her landing spot and only a spire, that she manages to grab, saves her from flying over the edge. Breezie seems to float in the wind, as he flies way past the edge of the roof, disappearing into the void, only to emerge minutes later by crawling back up. He explains that it took him a few seconds of sheer terror while free falling before realizing that he had very sticky fingers that adhere to anything. This happened halfway down when he secured his hands to a wall. Greenie breaks through a roof made of glass but recovers in the same sticky fashion. Yet bouncing roof to roof soon comes to an end.

"Guys, time to go and chase the shadows," Reddish commands.

We move and jump with ease through the skyline towards the place where we last saw shadows jumping. Once there, we scout the place and its surroundings. Faintly and directly underneath, we hear voices rumbling accompanied with music that sounds like a party celebration.

"What is that?" Breezie asks pointing at the ground.

"It looks like a scarf," answers Greenie picking it up.

"Pure silk," Reddish adds while caressing it with her cheeks.

"Where were they dropping from? There is no ledge here, it's just an enormous roof on an incline," Firee observes.

"It's nothing but a bare city rooftop with spires," Checkered confirms.

The moment she says these words, we all look at each other. I walk towards the location where we found the scarf. It's the exact spot where the shadows were dropping earlier and as all of the others watch in expectation, I pull the spire next to it. Instantly a black hole appears right in front of us. It's filled with swirling currents of electricity, sparking intense purple, blue, white, and yellow colors. It does not take long or a second thought though for us, one after the other to drop, with our arms tightly pressed to our sides, the way the shadows did, into the void. That's when our new quest begins.

Chapter 3

"The Jester"

I can't see a thing. All I know is that I am falling in slow motion. The glow in the distance is at first like a nodule far underneath me. As I drop further its intensity increases until I see myself descending into a loud, noisy hall, filled with smoke, and packed with people, some sitting on long wooden benches, others actually dancing on top of the matching tables. The place seems like a Bavarian "Biergarten" absent spirits, as the signs clearly warn that no alcohol is served, only potions, three hundred plus of them according to the gigantic menu posted on the huge back wall. I descend gently to the ground and soon thereafter, my five harlequin mates do the same. Apparently, our arrival is either irrelevant or perhaps just not noticed by the crowd. The music has a medieval touch to it. An excited, rather eccentric set of musicians play an organ, a lute, a harpsichord, a clavichord, an ensemble of violas, shawms, cornets, sackbuts, and all play monotonous tunes from another era. Yet the festivity radiates on everyone's face enjoying a rowdy boisterous party.

We move around marveling at the human menagerie in front of us.

"Nothing is what it seems," I remind myself of The Orloj's words.

Sure, enough as I examine more closely, I notice all kinds of weird things are happening; people levitating, dishes and cups flying, the snapping of fingers followed by things appearing or vanishing, and the constant flow of people dropping in or shuttling back up the black hole. The same group of young girls that we saw earlier, wearing dresses from the Victorian era, wave at us as we approach.

"Young wizard apprentice wannabes. How quaint," one of them mutters as we are appraised by the lot.

"What's the occasion?" I inquisitively take the initiative.

The group of young girls focus on us with mischievous eyes. They whisper in each other's ears and giggle among themselves until one of them finally speaks up.

The young girl explains, "at the square during the anniversary days for those deceased and honored, wizard visitors from all over the world get together at the city underneath the city, the alternate world."

"You mean, a wizards gathering that we can call a happening?"

"Exactly," an enchanting voice responds, as the girls are distracted by a group of hyper-dancers that individually lift them up, one by one and carry the rowdy girls to the dance floor.

This time, the familiar frantic buzz of the tiny batting wings shoots right next to my ears. I turn back and for the first time see the little —flying bugger— that hovers right in front of me. With my slightest movement it reacts backing away from me. I could swear, at least that's my feeling that in as much as

I am staring at it; it is staring right back at me.

"What do you want?" I inquire.

No response or reaction as it hovers in my proximity with the same annoying buzz.

"We are supposed to find statues and instead all we find is a flying insect," I declare with disdain.

As I speak it continues to hover in the same exact spot. I begin to turn away disregarding its presence and almost miss it. There is a tiny ray, an impossibly thin green laser, beaming out of the flying bug and directed at one particular patron. I turn around gazing at the individual who has the tiny laser beam touching his back and see for the second time, the old man with the bent top hat.

Then, I hear the following words. "Blunt, Buggie is responding to your desire." says Reddish, —the harlequin girl from Spain giving -right away- a name to the flying bugger. "I suspect that the old man could be our second statue," she surmises.

While walking towards the old man, I bow to Buggie in gratitude and the volume of its buzz seems to acknowledge this by increasing its intensity. The man with the bent top hat is narrating a tale that has his small audience captivated. He rubs his hands, his deft fingers in the air drawing imaginary figures. One of those is a circle forming exactly what appears, a small globe glowing with blinding intensity, floating between the palms of his hands, and following them. Then, as he shows it to everyone, he focuses on me.

"Sir, we are...," I start to address him, only to be immediately interrupted.

"I know who you are, Ujm! You got here a lot faster than I expected. Never mind, follow me," he says while hastily closing his act and marching out in a cacophonous storm of electric sparks.

We all are walking behind him when he makes a sweeping movement with his right hand and in an instant, we find ourselves walking through dark, empty city streets. At first sight everything seems the same, but it isn't! Every pamphlet on the ground or billboard on the walls, every shop and tavern sign is catered to wizards, sorcerers, enchanters, conjurers, or illusionists. "Same city, alternate world," with caution I remind myself, as I —and my fellow harlequins— trot behind the man with the bent top hat.

The old man picks up his pace and immediately disappears after turning left onto a dark alley. The six of us now follow walking through an impossibly narrow alleyway. Fog engulfs us and our visibility is quickly reduced to just a few yards in front of us. Soon, we exit onto a riverside street and the night sky is visible once more.

"There he goes," says Greenie, —the harlequin girl from Lebanon, while pointing to a tree lined pedestrian boulevard, and sure enough, in the distance we get a glimpse of the old man with the bent top hat.

He turns around and with an impatient gesture waves at us to speed it up. We all start trotting over the cobblestones in his direction, but he doesn't slow down, and not catching up we once again lose track of him. As we turn onto the street corner where we last saw him, six strangely looking individuals are blocking our way. They appear to have been waiting for us. We halt right in our track as they seem menacing enough to avoid.

"Where do you think you are going?" One of them challenges us as we are encircled.

"We are following the man with the bent top hat," I respond.

The pack surrounding us consists of a peculiar group encompassing six grown men. They are rather short in stature since they are not taller than any of us. They have protuberating heads, short club legs and even smaller arms.

Peering at us, their leader breaks out into a mischievous smile, and pointing as he slowly draws a circle with the palm of his hand, I involuntarily turn in the air until he has me upside down with my head less than an inch off the ground. He then performs the same magic on each of my startled harlequin mates.

Now, we're transformed and from my awkward position, I can see that we are all, once again wearing our normal everyday clothes. Mr. Kraus' words resonate in my head once more describing his upside-down world fable.

'Your harlequin personas will disappear when in contact with any of the six statues and you are genuinely at work on the three virtues or the three flaws,' I remind myself of the words as I recall The Orloj's instructions.

Then another memory flashes by...

I continue to recall Mr. Kraus' words, still not knowing quite how to react. "...What you are about to experience, is a world where everything will be upside down..."

One of them again asks as I take notice of his moniker, "why are you following the jester?"

"He was pointed out to us," I reply.

"Simply that's it! Is that the only reason you can think of and articulate?" He asks incredulously.

For the moment, I don't know how to answer.

"By the way, who pointed him out to you?" The dwarf asks.

I am embarrassed and afraid to answer.

Firee unhesitatingly replies without shyness, "a tiny flying bug."

"A bug?" They all in laugh in unison, mocking us.

"A bug! Is that the reason you are following him? Your group doesn't seem to be ready for this," he declares seemingly ready to end our quest.

"Holdup! Wait a minute miniscule man, I've got it. I've got it," Reddish intervenes.

Silence ensues. By his glare at her, it is obvious that the small man doesn't appreciate being referred to in that way.

He impatiently states, "I am waiting my lady, speak up, elaborate."

Reddish declares decisively, "We are following the man with the bent old hat because he may be one of the three statues of virtue, or one of the three statues of vice. We must meet him so as to master the virtue or learn from the flaw that he may possess. He may or may not represent these human characteristics, but we are keen to find out."

"Besides, we must be on the right track since our harlequin clothes have disappeared. The Orloj told us that this will happen only when we are genuinely in sync when working with the statues discovering the three virtues or the three flaws," I declare, supplementing Reddish observations.
No sooner than I complete my sentence, we are all gently deposited on the ground.

"Now, that's what we were waiting for. You clearly articulated what's motivating you. See, in life, we should always seek to know the reasons behind why we do what we do," their leader says these words and poof! Within the blink of an eye, the menacing bunch is gone.

The frantic buzz of the tiny batting wings approaches us through the fog until it hovers right above our heads. Then, as it starts to move forward, we obediently follow as it leads us through a labyrinth of narrow streets and alleyways until finally, we enter a small dead-end street housing a couple of broken streetlamps. At that moment —Buggie— points its tiny green laser towards the store front."

Tentatively, we open the door, and we peek inside, literally one head climbing over the other. We call out for our elusive antiquarian but get no response. Driven by sheer curiosity we step into the main hall of an antique bookstore built entirely out of dark decaying wood. It is covered in dust, giving off a strong scent of ancient paper and old leather. Dim lighting and scattered piles of books everywhere offer a dull ambience to the space.

'Their preferred occupation is that of antiquarians,' I remind myself of The Orloj words.

Without salutations we hear his voice bellowing from the shadowy back room.

"Have a seat you all. Call me Lazarus Zeetrikus with emphasis on the double ee," he commands.

'Double spelling? What is he talking about? Can I trust this man?' I wonder how productive this encounter can be, 'we need to focus on our objectives,' I conclude.

From my right, the familiar whisper of a voice arises once more. There he appears, Thumbpee, sitting comfortably at an angle that forces me to twist and turn my neck in order to see him. This time his yellow color is shiny, bright and his image crisp. He advises me "You can follow his guidance. Have an open mind and be without fear." He says these words as if reading my mind addressing my doubts in a flash before he disappears once again.

My thoughts are interrupted by the sound of Zeetrikus' high-pitched voice.

"Before you start asking me the same questions I hear repeatedly, let me ask and answer them for you. Am I a statue?

I am not saying that I am, that is for you to find out. But, if in fact, I transformed to be one, which of them am I? Well, that is also something for you to resolve," Lazarus —the old wizard— says.

"Let us begin with a reading that is quite applicable to your current circumstances," he announces.

"All of you quite often seem to be unhappy with, or bored of what you have, always yearning for the next thing you want to get and hold onto. Occasionally you seem to lack appreciation for all the good fortunes that you have," the old man with the bent top hat says rather solemnly as he continues lecturing us. "Let me think about, what would be the most appropriate and relevant book and subject for all of you?" He wrinkles his forehead, wrings his hands while pondering, as he paces around us in short steps that release brief bursts of energy.

Without another word he walks away, disappearing behind the rows and rows of ancient books. When he returns, our senses are all alert at full throttle. We can perceive every sound in the store, like the wood floor creaking as he walks back and forth, the furniture and shelves near him moving and grunting as he passes, a window that incessantly opens and closes pushed and pulled by the wind, the cuckoo clock that announces the turn of the hour and a couple of sparking neon lights that sound as if they are in need of urgent replacement.

The old man comes back with an ancient book, already open at the preselected page. "Here I have an ancient scribble, that is exacting as to what is afflicting you all," he says these words with a grin on his face as he starts to read in earnest.

"The Kite Flier and the Wise Old Master"

With the snow-capped Himalayas as a backdrop,
the wise old master,
though he seems restless and uneasy,
still exudes the awareness of a focused good observer.

He has closely cropped white hair,
a round face with a sparse moustache,
a tiny mouth with barely noticeable lips,
intense eyes filled with serenity and wisdom.

The boy,
he is keeping an eye on,
flies a kite reaching high up into the sky,
bright and shiny colors it has,
swirls with the winds of Annapurna,
climbs in a frenzy and dives in every direction,
at the mercy of its diminutive handler.

"It is never fast enough," complains the little boy
with a grin on his face.

Suddenly,
the winds from the menacing mountain
arrive and the show is over quickly.

"Another dud," protests the boy from Nepal,
as he picks-up his crashed papier mâché,
flying object.

Standing at the doorstep of his modest residence,

the wise old master is not pleased.

The young boy comes running and sits
on the rocky dirt,
beside his mentor.

"Let me take a look at your kite," the Wisemaster says.

With quick and highly skilled movements,
in no time,
the craftsman's hands tinker, cut and paste,
rendering the kite in top shape,
ready in no time to fly again.

The youth bows in gratitude
at the stern face of the old master.

"Try it now, Tenzing," he commands.

The young boy quickly runs away
against the wind
while deftly pulling the strings.

The kite promptly soars,
higher and faster than ever before,
it rides the winds of the mountain of heaven,
with ease,
drawing perfectly elliptical paths,
and wide circles,
on its wake.

But once again, the boy does not smile,

much less so his wise mentor.

"All other kites at our village
are either faster or better than mine,"
he blurts out while talking to himself.

"Besides,
for all of us,
the kids of this town,
it is pointless to fly kites,
against the winds of the monster mountain."

"Tenzing come over here!"
demands the exasperated Wisemaster.

After picking-up his, once again, newly smashed kite,
the young boy runs right to his mentor's doorstep.

"What is it with your restless soul?" the old master asks.

"My kite is useless," responds the young Nepalese boy.

He wears a frustrated expression,
while standing next to his broken and inert flying object
lying on the dirt.

"We'll see about that," the wise man asserts.

After repairing the kite,
while deftly pulling the strings,
he takes a few quick steps,
instantly lifting the kite into the blue sky.

Like an arrow piercing through the air,
the kite flies at a frantic pace,
at gravity defying angles,
perilously dangerous curves,
lopsided turns,
jet engine elevators,
speed of light simulators.

"Wisemaster, how can you do it?"
The Nepalese youngster asks,
as the old man continues to pilot the kite
as if it were on a racetrack.

Kite on his shoulder,
its tail being dragged behind,
with the freezing winds of Annapurna now howling,
the young Sherpa walks alongside the wise old man,
as they head towards the mountain temple,
where their daily mentoring sessions take place.

"Tenzing, you missed the magnificent flight of your kite,"
the Wisemaster observes while adding,
"You were concentrating within your mind so much
on the imperfections,
that the joyful ride totally escaped you."

"Master, what should I have done then?" Asks the perplexed
young boy.

"Do not obsess any longer on what you are lacking
but only on what you do have,

whatever that is,"
the Wisemaster replies.

"Immersed in your never-ending grievances,
you are not enjoying the journey," he continues.

The old man paces with pensive strides.

"Look up!" He suddenly commands while the young boy
jumps in obedience.

"See, glorious, cloudless skies.
A gift, a privilege to be enjoyed.
In life as we march along,
it is rewarding when we are aware
of our surroundings,
and paying attention.
It evidently is worth it to view the sides,
and both before and behind,
because at every turn,
there are lofty existential treasures
waiting for us at every turn,"
the Wisemaster adds.

"Now breath deep,"
the old man orders the young man.

Tenzing does as instructed,
filling his lungs with fresh air.

"You see, while you argue and complain
which constricts your veins,

not enough oxygen is inhaled,
to pump life into your being,"
notes the wise old master.

Tenzing lowers his head in embarrassment,
but the wise man is not done yet.

"My beloved mentee,
you always find the need to compare yourself
or what you have.
the kites of others are always better than yours.
You constantly aspire for
what others are or have,
hence, you are perennially unhappy,
deeply in fact,"
states the old man in a reflective trance.

"But there is an additional existential disease
that rots your insides,
including your spirit and soul:
Excuses and more excuses.
Today you blamed the mountain's winds,
but all you did was to complain
trying to hide your lack of mastery."

"Your kite piloting skills are limited.
You denigrate your kite so often and so much,
that you are never in a position
to extract the most out of what it can do.
You complain and protest so frequently,
while operating it,
that you fail to study, learn, and practice,

which are the only ways to advance in life.
Hence, there is no progress for you as a pilot.
Your lack of mastery is a consequence
of your lack of effort,
that condemns one to a life of mediocrity,"
the emotional Wisemaster adds.

"I've just flown your kite.
What was the difference between you and me?
After all it was the same kite,
the same weather and the same location,"
the old man emotionally exclaims.

The young apprentice reacts,
"You were totally focused on the moment, therefore able to
extract the most out of my kite."

The Wisemaster remarks in exaltation, "Exactly!"

"You enjoyed the flight, the kite, the surroundings
and above all you enjoyed the journey,
even though,
you were aware that none of them were perfect,"
responds the suddenly inspired young man.

"Wonderful! You're beginning to understand," states a
jubilant old man.

"You paid no attention to appearances,
neither kites others may have,
much less the trying weather,"
concludes the smiling young man,

"Tenzing, you are now ready to become a master of what
you love to do. Go, go, and enjoy the ride," states the
Wisemaster.

The young Nepalese boy runs with his kite;
when ready, still holding the strings,
he releases it to fly,
high up into the sky,
it sails masterfully,
with a now deft touch.
The biggest triumph though,
is that he wears a bright big wide smile,
that goes along quite fittingly,
with the magnificent event he's experiencing
while maneuvering his kite
in front of his venerable mentor.

The man with the bent top hat observes us as if he were the
Wisemaster. He has our absolute attention. As he paces back
and forth, he formulates his first question for us.

"What does the flight of a kite symbolize to you all?"

"Fun and speed, sir," replies Greenie.

"What about freedom?" he offers.

"That as well," I reply.

"It also resembles our life's journey," he adds.

"Why?" Reddish asks.

"The kite is our journey's craft. It is magnificently
beautiful but needs tinkering and preparation before it's ready
to fly. It doesn't fly by itself though. We need to cause forward
movement dragging it from behind for it to take-off. Once in
the air it is in a constant tug of war against the elements but

the rewards are lofty and commensurate with our skills and goals. With absolute control of the strings, the quality of the flight is entirely up to our skills, knowledge, fortitude, nerve, and guts. And yes, almost inevitably, eventually we will return back down to earth, sometimes in need of attention and repairs, then only to turn around and fly up, up, again and again."

The mysterious and elusive Lazarus Zeetrikus' elucidation serves to navigate our understanding of the events so far. We all gaze at him in amazement while working to connect the dots.

"We all have the opportunity and choice to similarly fly our own kites of life. It is entirely up to us. If any or all of you visualizes this parable, keep in mind the pitfalls, as the wise old master pointed out to Tenzing, the Nepalese boy that demonstrated this kind of existential endeavor and challenge," he concludes.

"Mr. Zeetrikus, what about the clues?" Asks an incredulous Breezie, —the harlequin boy from China.

"What about them?" Retorts the man with the bent top hat.

"Is this story connected to them?" Breezie presses.

"I don't know, you tell me. Which of the virtues or flaws do you think this encounter and discussion relates to?" The old man responds rhetorically.

At first none of us keenly attentive six harlequins know how to answer.

"During your quest you have to be proactive, ready to ask and answer that question in order to advance, otherwise you'll find yourselves immobile," the older man warns us.

"I'll volunteer to say pride, because the Nepalese kid was too proud to ask for help or advice," Reddish says.

That's when I have an epiphany.

"To expand on that, the other choice will be humility as the Nepalese kid's pride, at first caused his failure to recognize and respect the vast knowledge of his mentor, therefore he missed the opportunity to learn from him," I explain.

"Aren't the two arguments for pride and humility one and the same, just two sides of the same coin?" Asks Zeektrikus, the antiquarian. "One needs to incorporate humility in our character in order to learn and admit our mistakes, but in order to achieve this, one needs to keep pride under control, as it can impede and destroy honesty with oneself."

Through a portal he opens with a snap of the fingers, the antiquarian walks us back to the medieval tavern and dancing hall and as he's ready to part ways, I have one more question to ask of him.

"What do we call you sir?" I ask him as he turns demonstrating a mischievous face.

"The Jester, that's what everyone calls me."

"We all knew that one." For a change I chuckle inside, knowing something the man with the bent top hat doesn't.

"Do you have a clue for our quest?" Reddish asks.

"Actually, I don't"

Breezie presses, "Where can we find one?"

"That's for you to figure out, besides I can't talk to you any further about the subject," he says this as he turns and in a fraction of a second, he is gone.

Firee —the harlequin boy from India, wonders aloud, "what do we do now?"

"I believe we need to understand what the message of the story is, in order to know how to proceed," I answer.

As we start to walk along the dark cobblestones in the "alternate" Prague's world of wizards, we can hear for the third time, originating from around the corner, familiar laughter. It's from the boisterous group of young girls wearing Victorian dresses. As I see them, a nagging feeling forms a question that pops in my head.

"Why do we keep running into them?"

Showing up unannounced again, my little conscience whispers from my shoulder, "Erasmus you have to be weary and careful around these young girls."

"Why?"

"They are rated the best group of working pickpockets there are in this city."

"Pickpockets?"

"Right! They will try to steal the clues that you find. At this moment, all they are doing is sizing you up and verifying whether or not you've already discovered any clues."

"Why would they want to steal them?"

"They themselves want to become wizards."

I contemplate my conscientious speck of a man with disbelief and respect. In other words, even as I'm thoughtful, I'm very confused.

"One more thing, only this time, you'll know your headed into trouble when once again you're dressed in the harlequin personas and clothes." My diminutive conscience warns me by offering this advice.

I look at myself and sure enough, I am back again as a blue harlequin and once again in the blink of an eye, Thumbpee is gone!

"Our handsome boys are back," one of the young women announces this as she in short half-circles, walks towards us. I control my urge to call out to them, and simply whisper at my companions to keep walking and pass right by them.

"Have a nice evening ladies. I am sure we'll be seeing you along the way, now though, we are in a hurry," I say politely but firmly.

We struggle trying to find a spot where we can review, debate, and consider our visit with the Jester in order to figure out, whether through him, we have gained a path to one more clue. As we pass on by, they mock and ridicule us. The young women in Victorian dresses are obviously not the least pleased with us. Nevertheless, the six of us ignore and leave them behind. Surprisingly, we are again dressed in regular street clothes indicating that we are back on track in pursuit of our mission to the get the second clue.

In the meantime, the rowdy Victorian bunch morph into their usual selves becoming the menacing figures of the night. They are always watching from the rooftops and ledges in the city of Prague, their riveting maleficent eyes focused intensely on everything and everyone in their sight.

"Ok, ok, I get it," mutters Reddish unintelligibly.

Buggie's buzz makes itself present once more, as he hovers around a bronze statue of a man on a horse. It is the figure of a noble man on the move. We all look at it, at first incredulously, but as we gaze at the imposing figure, a rising uncomfortable gut feeling starts to build up. My mates experience the same, showing expressions of awe and wonder that are discernable on each of their faces.

"His eyes are alive," observes Breezie as we all realize what is actually happening.

"Guys, is this our second clue?" Reddish asks the question while sounding uncertain and a bit lost.

"I don't know, but we'll soon find out," I state this with an instinctive assuredness that we must be close, really, really close."

"You always say that," says Greenie.

The statue of the horseman and his beautiful stallion are on the move.

"Wait, wait!" I shout out as the statue begins to mobilize and march forward.

"Humility allows us to be open minded, practice reciprocating and learning, but we need to also control our pride, so it does not stand in the way and blinds us," I blurt out quoting without thinking the words of the man with the bent old hat.

Breezie adds, "pride not only blinds but it also can send us in the wrong direction."

Buggie's buzz erupts, and its pace is frantic. He circles above us instead of hovering, his flight is erratic with sudden bursts. As we all contemplate him, the flying bug unexpectedly stops in midair and points his tiny laser at the ground.

The six of us turn our heads towards the cobblestone street, and gaze at the now empty spot. At first, we see nothing, but then, the rumbling starts; faintly at first, it rapidly grows in intensity and sound. In that very same place, an intense light appears as a tiny dot, then expands into a sphere of sparkling brightness and soaring colors. It soon blinds us, until the balloon of light simply bursts into shining dust that in slow motion rains down to the ground.

"What is that?" Checkered —the harlequin girl from South-Africa, is pointing at the cobblestones.

Right then and there we see a single envelope on the floor. I take a step forward. Out of the eyes of the departing equestrian statue, a couple of rays of light beam to the ground creating a ring of fire around the envelope. The sculpted horseman is without notice gone, and our hearts sink. While flames intensely grow, the circle of fire rapidly closes on the envelope. I stand paralyzed, not knowing what to do until in a snap, I remember the words of my tiny conscience.

"Now, you can walk through fire and ice."

I gather the courage, swallow hard and simply walk through the fire and pick up the envelope. It reads, "Pride," and has a note written next to the word: "With compliments, well done apprentices! Yours truly, The Jester."

"Was he the horseman?" Firee asks rhetorically.

"Yes! That was the wicked Lazarus Zeetrikus a statue of flaw," affirms Reddish.

"No wonder," I voice aloud jumping in celebration and everyone nodding in agreement acknowledges this understanding.

I turn around and wave at my fellow harlequins. Once more they form a pile on top of me. In the meantime, the most inquisitive of our group, now with two clues in hand, Reddish cannot contain herself and opens the envelopes. She immediately starts to read aloud.

"...The tunnel's door lies underneath the old scribble, through the trickling river, past your worst fears..."

The words are in the envelope containing the clue of Humility.

The rest of us turn around and ask her to read it again. To no avail we are lost, as we don't have the foggiest idea what the clue means. Again, without hesitating for feedback, Reddish reads the second clue.

Reddish now, reviews the clue of Pride.

The tiny but familiar weight on my shoulder announces to me that Thumbpee has returned.

"Don't try to decipher the meaning of the clues at this time."

"To ask why, would be foolish, right?" I clumsily ask, trying to be sardonic.

"No, it's actually, a very good question. It is pointless to do so at this time, because you require other clues in order to understand the meaning of these two."

Firee asks, "what is our new power?"

"The ability of one of you at a time, to know when someone is lying!" The diminutive conscience explains this new power before again vanishing.

We all look at each other and know exactly what to do next. It is me though, the only one of us to recall and verbalize the exact words given to us by the powerful clock.

"Every time you are in possession of a couple of clues, you earn the right to come over and ask me for further guidance, insight and wisdom."

Since no one reacts, I take the initiative.

"Guys, it's time to go and consult with The Orloj," I say this realizing our collective view of helplessness. When everyone consents, we are on our way without hesitation.

Chapter 4

"Never Enough Time"

As dawn approaches, we enter Staromestske Namesti (the Old Town Square). The six of us head towards The Orloj's tower. As we walk, the now familiar but still annoying buzz of Buggie's frantic flapping wings joins us, as the sound hovers just above our heads. In a flash, I can feel Thumbpee on my shoulder as he has obviously invited himself to the occasion.

The large ancient old clock is waiting for us. As soon as we stand in front of the old clock, it comes to life and its thunderous voice is immediately felt.

"Well done! You are now in possession of two clues, one human virtue and one human flaw."

"Sir, we need your help so that we can figure out the clues," interjects Reddish.

The Orloj responds rather cryptically, "I can't help you solve the clues."

We look at him puzzled.

I recall that he told to us to come and see him every time we had two clues in hand. The Orloj seems to read my mind.

"I've been assisting you all the way."

Breezie asks, "if I may, Sir, please clarify how you have done so?"

The ancient clock amusingly responds, "Through my sons."

"Well, as far as I'm concerned, they've been nowhere to be seen. Perhaps this is a case of dereliction of duty, and they simply are distracted or partying somewhere else." A rather sarcastic Firee responds aggressively.

The Orloj is not bemused.

"They have been with you all the way." He projects authority with his thunderous voice.

Incredulously we all look at one another. Doing so, we take account of all those present, noticing our companions. We all catch on in tandem, expressing ourselves with an exclamation of joy.

"Buggie and Thumbpee!" We all shout in chorus while laughing about it.

"Ahem, ahem, ahem." The ancient clock clears his throat trying to catch our attention. "Is there anything I can help you with?" He asks this teasingly leaving it up to us to decisively figure out in which way he can help.

"Sir, you mentioned the statues of flaws as dangerous and that they could steer us in the wrong direction. However, that didn't occur with Mr. Lazurus Zeetrikus," Greenie — the harlequin girl from Lebanon, points out.

"That's not correct. When you all were with him you did incur a couple of dangerous obstacles and detours. You faced and navigated them with ease, demonstrating flexibility, imagination and most importantly, in every instance you listened well, knew how to take advice and when to be decisive. So far kids, you've demonstrated, flawless judgment. Kudos to you all!" The Orloj proudly voices this praise.

'We came here seeking advice, not another lecture.' I think about his words growing impatient by the minute.

"But I don't anticipate the quest for —wizardry apprenticeship graduation— to continue to be this easy." The Orloj cautions, preparing us for the next stage of advancement.

Checkered asks, "Sir, what's your advice at this point?"

"Be aware of the liars and cheats, they will not be easy to detect. Also, now that your quest continues in daylight, remember that in the alternate world you find yourselves, there's light in the darkness and there's darkness in the light," he pontificates mysteriously before he adds a couple of encouraging parting words. "Whether by chance or fate, you've been provided two pillars of knowledge. Humility which is a virtue to embrace and pride which is a flaw to avoid. I can see no better foundation underlying the path ahead of you." Concluded, he just goes back into hibernation.

Once again, The Orloj's withdrawal leaves we six clueless kids without knowing exactly what to do next. As usual, Thumbpee and Buggie are nowhere to be found either.

Breezie —the harlequin boy from China, announces, "these two come and go as they please, their presence is not up to us?"

Greenie responds that it is not entirely up to them. "The Orloj said that when in need we can just summon them."

Thanks to Firee, we come to the realization, "guys, just in case you haven't noticed, at this pace, we don't have enough time to obtain the four remaining clues and embark on the navigation of the tunnel. We have to pick-up our pace, otherwise we'll fail."

The six of us walk through Staromestske Namesti (The Old Town Square) with the light of a new dawn just breaking. In the horizon it is illuminating our target, the intimidating and unsettling Hradcany Castle (Prague's castle) located on the hill across the river. As we approach the pedestrian boulevard of Vaclavske Namesti (Wenceslas' Square), the facades and walls are too inviting for our sticky suits. It doesn't take long for the six of us to observe the city life while hanging from the sides of the buildings. Oddly enough, the strange characters walking through the boulevard are not at all surprised to see a group of colorful harlequins, staring at them from the walls, ledges, and windows of the boulevard. We keep on going climbing up until once again we reach the rooftops. Now the boulevard looks much smaller but still by no means appears normal.

"What are all of those colors that are exiting all of those buildings?" Reddish —the harlequin girl from Spain, is concerned.

A few blocks away in the distance, gigantic colorful flags can be seen partially jutting out of the rooftops. Using the spires as springs, we hop from roof to roof, until we reach the display. We can see another pedestrian street beneath us and this one is adorned with street performers plus a couple of music bands. To one of its sides there are rows and rows of street vendors. With caution we descend down the walls reaching a high first story level.

It doesn't take long for us to realize that neither its patrons nor the street market are normal or what you'd expect. The characters that surround us seem to have been extracted out of a circus. Descending to the street level, we stroll around the acts of magic, acrobats, and mimes and that's when for the first time we see the sign.

"Van Egmond Book Antiquarians"
(Est. as Old as this City is)

Swiftly we all poise outside the shop until I take the lead and the rest follow.

We all step inside and immediately realize that our clothes have transformed back to "normal." This gives us confidence, causing us to be even more alert and aware of our surroundings.

The gentle, senior-citizens lady with long, threaded white hair sits on a rocking chair. She has pale skin and fine features, including an aquiline nose and milky blue eyes; her long and wide skirt reaches her ankles, and her shirt sleeves hug her wrists. She is reading what appears to be a very old book, but sensing us, lifts her eyes and gives us a warm welcoming smile.

"Ah! The young aspiring wizard apprentices."

She stands up and comes over to greet us with a soft shake of the hands and a light kiss on both cheeks. She is of average size but towering in height. At about two meters, she's pretty tall. Pointing to the tray on top of a chest drawer, "welcome to my humble shop, my name is Lucrecia Van Egmond." Say effusive, while keenly observing each one of us.

Promptly after our cursory introduction and the demonstrative warmth of her greeting, her protective and reassuring grandmotherly demeanor makes us feel totally safe and protected.

"You must all be hungry. Help yourselves to a sumptuous breakfast." She continues with her calm and sweet tone of voice, that instantly puts all of us even more at ease.

While each of us gulp hearty portions of the morning meal, she gets right down to business.

"I hear you are making very good progress on your quest." Her eyes are inquisitive, waiting for a response.

"In a way yes, but we have yet to grasp firm exact footing of what we are doing."

"Well, my dear youngsters, many of our quests in life lack solid ground, definition or even clarity. We have to be prepared for life's journeys that can be sometimes like this. We are challenged to thrive in chaos and unpredictability so the paths we traverse lack firm ground. When in life we learn to move forward without solid footing underneath, we become experts in navigating the moving sands. In those shifting circumstances it is easy to dismiss or abandon the quest due to a lack of support or rationale behind them." Her reasoning feels like a sermon, but we all are more interested in the meal than in her insightful words.

Mrs. Van Egmond paces the floor until her face lights up.

"All of you follow me, we are going to take a walk in the backwoods of Prague." She marches towards the back of the shop trailed by the six of us who are wondering if we are going to be walking through a dark and ominous forest.

The tall antiquarian stands in front of her store's backdoor that is painted in multiple pastel colors. Before opening it, she bunches all of us together, holding our intertwined hands in front of it. Turning the door handle in slow motion she conjures something incomprehensible through her clenched teeth. The moment the door starts to open, an intense and blinding light filters through it.

Mrs. Van Egmond steps into and together we all follow her into what is a totally different venue. How wrong we were to anticipate a dark forest awaiting us. We find ourselves actually on a countryside landscape, at the edge of a forest with not a cloud in the bright sky. It is the middle of a glorious day. Far in the distance we can see Prague's skyline.

"Let's get moving." Mrs. Van Egmond starts to walk into the forest and dutifully we once more follow her lead.

With agile steps she leads us deep into the foliage. Rays of light filter through the tall trees as we are immersed more and more in the sounds, scents, and colors of nature. A small creek makes itself present. We walk alongside its edge until we reach an open clearing amongst the trees.

The old antiquarian asks us to sit down and form a circle.

"We are here today to talk about where in our world we can find the best example of a giving heart. The problem with generosity is that it isn't recognized, appreciated, valued, or respected enough. The ultimate boundless example of generosity is found in nature. I have brought with me a scribble that depicts lucidly what generosity means." She commences reading in earnest.

"The Old Man and Mother Nature"

While a new day begins
in between the jagged edges
of the snowcapped mountains,
the sun breaks in the horizon.

The old man drags himself up
step by step
as he grudgingly labors
up the steep mountain hike.

Every one of his bones
makes creaking noises

hurting as he moves.

A beautiful forest surrounds him
while the path he follows
zig zags endlessly through the slow climb.

His little sac bounces on his back,
his precious midway meal lies in there.

The steep terrain opens up
as he leaves the dense foliage behind.

The landscape is now a plateau
composed of mountain peaks
illustrating the background.

While he ascends
over a narrow way of loose flat stones,
the terrain is carpeted
with wildflowers and kneecap grass.

Above him there isn't a single cloud in the sky
but only intense and stunning hues of blue
acting as his heavenly ceiling.

The summit is the reward
for an effort that has lasted for many hours.

At the top of the mountain lies a deep blue lake,
on its side lies an elongated waterfall
that frames and trickles into it.

On his back he can see the valley where he started.
The panoramic alpine views
allow him to see a blurry image
of his village from afar,
miles and miles away.

"I am short of breath
and my mouth is so dry,
I can hardly swallow."
He announces seemingly to no one.

"Besides, my runny nose and watery eyes
are trying to tell me
that my allergies are running amuck."
he continues talking all to himself
as he walks towards the top.

Then, as always happens,
the thunderous voice permeates all over,
the sound waves can be felt everywhere.

"How do you like the smell of the forest
you are climbing?"
Asks mother nature of the old man.

"Same as always,
but right now, I'm gasping for air
afflicted by my summer allergies."
He answers with a cranky voice.

"Discomfort is compensated by a gorgeous day
and the stunning colors

of the flowers, butterflies, autumn leaves
and a clear blue sky all around you."
Nature counters.

"From you, as expected,
besides, what good is it?
So much beauty if I can't enjoy it."
Is the cursory answer from the old man.

"What about the sounds of the wind
brushing and whistling through the trees,
the birds singing,
the tiny creek's waters
coursing through downstream,
the wicked Jiminy Crickets
seemingly unlimited,
all members of my perennial open-air orchestra."
Mother nature argues.

"What do you want from me, nature?
Don't you understand that I am having a hard time?
Or is it that you just want me
to magically forget it all
just thinking and feeling
only about 'the nice things in life?'"
The exasperated old man argues back.

"Precisely, privileged man."
Nature bellows in a stern voice.

"Privileged, are you kidding me?"
He counters with sarcasm.

"Your good health and enduring strength
have made it possible for you to climb
this tough and challenging terrain
all the way to this beautiful summit!"
Unfazed, mother nature counters.

Responsively,
"why don't you leave alone
my sorrowfulness and foul mood.
You are not going to persuade me
to cheer up when I don't feel like it."
He attempts,
blocking the uncomfortable weight
of a reality he doesn't want to see or feel.

"You've earned the privilege
to be standing at the pinnacle of the world
with this backdrop of stunning views
all around you
and yet somehow, you've found a way
to be unhappy about it,
worst of all,
not even appreciating it."
Mother nature rebuts
in a solemn and stern voice.

The old man remains silent
trying to show
indifference, but his eyes
are attentive and seem to
be pleading
to mother nature,
not to give up on him.

"Old man what if
the air you breath
that I provide for you
every second you are alive,
is suddenly gone?
Or what would happen
if the oceans, rivers, lakes, springs, and wells
were to dry out in an instant?
Or if the protective shield of our planet
were to vanish in a split second?
Why do you take for granted
that these boundless gifts
you receive everyday
will continue forever?
You have an existential obligation
to give back,
to life and others
for the privilege of being alive."
This is a declaration
by a visibly obfuscated mother nature.

The old man eyes are filled with intensity
as he's followed every word
mother nature has just uttered.

"And how do I do that?"
He babbles in embarrassment.

"In life we do that which has been
prescribed, obligated, and meant for us to do,
as participants
in the natural order of the universe."

"Sometimes we are at the receiving end,
others on the giving end."
Nature declares with profound wisdom.

"Your generosity unsettles me,
you make me feel uncomfortable around you."

"Perhaps guilty?" Counters nature.

"What does it matter how I feel?
but tell me please,
how can you do all that you do
without receiving anything in return
for your actions?"
An incredulous old man retorts.

"That is what being generous means.
It's about paying forward.
Being giving is not a choice,
it is a debt.
Our existential obligations keep piling up
as long as we remain
the beneficiaries of the privilege
of partaking in this earth."
Adds mother earth sounding calmer
as the attention of the older man rises.

"Be gracious, cheerful
and celebrate the life you enjoy
each and every day
and make it your existential purpose
to gratefully give back as much as you receive.

Don't cause me to change my mindset
and stop giving you all those things
that sustain your life.

Above all, be mindful that
my generosity comes
without any strings attached to it.
I never ask for anything
in return to offset what I give.

Hence, why shouldn't you as well
give back equally so?"

Mrs. Van Egmond finishes reading the document while we seem to be keenly aware of our surroundings as if we are searching for mother nature itself.

"Young harlequins, there is nothing in life more giving than nature itself. Let us pause for a second. I want all of you to close your eyes."

Silence follows as she deliberately remains mute, but not for long. The sound of the wind can be felt through the leaves. A cricket bursts like a strident horn repeating itself at random, a frog croaks along with it, as if an alternating chorus, but the main vocals are from the birds. The choir is without prompting playing non-stop, filling the air with magic and nature's beautiful symphony.

"We take nature for granted and we do so because it is always there. Here we are in the middle of a timeless forest and without asking anything of us, we are being provided with an avalanche of precious gifts. The air we breathe, the light we see, the scents we feel, the sounds we hear. They are all ours for simply being alive. But are we aware of the life bounty we have?" She pointedly asks us to see what she sees.

"What about in your own lives? Do you give yourself to others? Do you caringly provide good deeds to others in need without it being asked for, or are you expecting reciprocity in return?"

We all nod our heads as if finally comprehending the message.

"Being generous is not a choice, it's an obligation!" I suddenly say aloud without thinking "If I don't give back to life and others, eventually, everything will be lost or taken away from me."

The moment I utter these words, we are no longer seated in the midst of the forest but rather situated along the sidewalk of a busy Prague street. The noise brings us all back to the here and now. Mrs. Van Egmond is nowhere to be seen but her voice materializes filling the air.

"Young wizard apprentice candidates, you've learned an important lesson today."

Surprisingly, her translucent face appears in front of us floating in the air.

"Here you go, you've earned it. I wish you the best at your quest." She hands us a white envelope and with a slight gust she vanishes into the air.

It reads, Generosity.

Initially my first instinct is to read its contents at once but as I am about to quickly tear the envelope open, Thumbpee's voice surprises me once more. He sits on my right shoulder with his arms and legs crossed. His, is not a happy face whatsoever.

"Aren't you forgetting something?" He asks this with an admonishing tone and then smiles.

I look at him smiling back knowing full well what he's talking about.

"Shall we call it, youthful exuberance?"

"Remember the clues work best when opened in pairs," Thumbpee and I in sync recite this unchoreographed verse while bursting out in loud laughter.

"Harlequins, dangers await on the path ahead of you," the little man says before vanishing again.

"We have but just a few hours remaining to find the other statues. Let's get moving." I push everyone into the lively alternate version of the city of Prague. One that is filled in every walk of life with wizardry and sorcerers.

Our harlequin suits are back on, meaning that we are starting again from scratch.

Says an exalted Firee jumping up and down, "Thumbpee forgot all about it!"

We all turn around towards him showing perplexed faces.

"Forgot what?" I ask.

Unexpectedly, the spec of a man appears of my shoulder cutting into our conversation. "No, I haven't!" I've been observing and waiting for your decision while preparing the next steps." His hand is holding his chin as if he is nodding and admonishing us at the same time.

"So, explain yourself then." Firee —the harlequin boy from India, demands clarification, showing no patience for Thumbpee's nonsensical words.

"From now onwards you have the ability to create a portal. This power will rotate amongst yourselves and only one of you will possess it at any given time for that instance when you decide to use it, so long as the situation justifies it."

"A portal?" Greenie asks excited.

"An indiscernible doorway," explains the tiny man.

"Simply speaking, quickly swipe your right hand in front of you and a blurry translucent image of a wide door will appear before you. Only the six of you are able to walk through it. Simply step forward, enter and you will immediately emerge in a different area of the city."

"Do we have control of our destination?" Asks Breezie.

"Yes and no," says Thumbpee. "If you all have a clear, concise goal in mind, your intended location will be where you land, but if not, you'll emerge randomly anywhere in the city, even at unsavory and dangerous places."

And just like that. Thumbpee disappears in his usual way.

"Time to move on." I am assertive and we start to walk through the narrow streets of the magical city.

Chapter 5

"In Broad Daylight"

We are all fixated above the hill on the Hradcany Castle across the river Vltava. Even in broad daylight absent its constant radiant night illumination, the ancient structure reigns over the city.

Hurriedly Greenie is the first to act.

"Let's go to the castle right now."

Impulsively and without a thought or worry, she swipes her hand across the air from right to left and lucky her, the newest of all powers is in her control. The air in front of us becomes blurry and the translucent shape of a door slowly starts to form. Without asking, as I am about to tell her to halt, Greenie simply walks through it. After all, being curious children, as we see her literally disappear through the door, we all follow Greenie into the unknown.

In a flash, we find ourselves in the very same spot as before, but it is now nighttime and quite dark. It is a clear, starry, moonless night.

"I aimed for the castle. Sorry guys."

"If you all have a single clear, concise location in mind, your destination will be granted," Reddish —the harlequin girl from Spain, is critical of the impulsive act. "Obviously we weren't clear at all as you just jumped the gun on us." Greenie's apology is cut off.

"And you won't have the power back for a while, so don't even think it can immediately help you. It won't happen,"

Thumbpee informs us as he appears back on my shoulder but is quickly gone a moment later.

"See what has taken place. One impulsive bad decision, a wrong turn and things in a hurry turn for the worst," I say this, addressing everyone.

"We have to go back," says Firee countering back.

"Back to where?" Greenie asks.

"Daylight," replies Firee.

"Why?"

"Look at the clock. Pay attention to what time is it?" points out Firee.

We all turn around and see the giant clock on the side wall of an old building across the street. "8:00 PM," I say. "We've lost 10 of the 24 hours we were given to complete our quest." Everyone nods. "At least this time, we all seem to be in agreement about what our goal is."

We all, simultaneously, swipe our hands in the air and determine that our portal power has not yet returned back. Worst of all, we don't really know when it will! So, for the moment we are stuck here!

"What is that?" Breezie points our wondering.

That's when for the first time I see the flares in the night sky. Flashes of light unexpectedly inundate the darkness above us. Brush strokes of yellow, green, purple, and soft reds appear as bolts crisscross each other in a slow dance. Then, I remember the words of The Orloj and fear spreads quickly throughout my entire body.

"Be aware of the cosmic storms and the northern lights." When they are present it is an omen that serious trouble lies ahead.

"Blunt, what are you thinking about? All of sudden, you seem afraid," Reddish says as she as well looks up at the sky.

She gazes up focusing, watching, just for a second. She immediately turns bug-eyed, looking at me with intense eyes of fear.

"The..." she starts to say as we simultaneously finish the phrase together, "...northern lights."

"Let's get moving." I emphasize in haste.

That's when we hear the distant sounds of an orchestra. We all turn searching for the source and soon find ourselves facing the river darkness. As we hone into the approaching tune what we hear is the lively melody of a band with all sorts of instruments playing together. Through the river's fog, we can barely see the blurry simple images of a Christmas tree-like lights. Soon after, what comes into view are the silhouettes of parading large barges emerging through the misty fog, and quickly capturing our imagination as our surveillance freezes on it. There are living creatures of all colors riding on top of them, made up of greens, purples, blues, yellows, reds. They all seem to be having a ball, dancing, singing, laughing loudly, and jumping everywhere. Shiny musical instruments also come into view, clarinets, trumpets, drums, violins, pianos, and others. We focus our sights and are in for a big surprise. The figures partying and celebrating seem to be floating or flying through the air and they are translucent!

"Are those what I think they are?" Greenie wonders.

Right after her words are uttered, the barges' parade comes to a sudden halt as if having arrived at their destination. Then, a stampede begins. The colorful and transparent individuals fly out scattering in all directions through the city's night sky and to our horror a number of them head toward us.

"These must be the aspiring wizard apprentices." Right in front of us comments a flying blurry and purple figure that is dressed like a pirate and has rotten teeth.

"What are we supposed to do with them?" Asks a hovering and translucent yellowish figure that is dressed like a Victorian-era lady.

Both figures are joined by two others that appear even more menacing. They form a circle in the air, around us, threatening mayhem while seemingly trying to figure out their next move. Materializing apparently out of nowhere, I feel Thumbpee's presence on my shoulder.

"This is the annual parade of ghosts, lost spirits and wizard departed souls gathered from around the world. They always show up in the same manner, during the annual wizards and witches festivities held in Prague. They pop-up to disturb and disrupt the community." He whispers this explanation into my ear.

At that moment the six of us start to float and I see the yellowish spirit gesturing upwards with movements of her hands. Abruptly she moves forward. It is only when we are suspended in the air right above the frigid waters of the Vltava river that we begin to realize the seriousness of our situation.

A bluish figure dressed as a court jester inquisitively addresses us. "What are you up to youngsters?"

"We are in search of The Orloj's six statues," I reply revealing anxiety with the inflection of my voice.

"Hm… I see, but you failed to mention how come you are here tonight?" The court jester presses in a resonating voice.

We remain silent not knowing how to answer.

"For example, see how the impulsive act by one of you, has landed the entire gang here at this event." The transparent jester continues, "sometimes bad decisions carry significant consequences that change the course of our lives. The unresolved question before us now is, what fate is in store for all of you?"

The flying spirits giggle when they see our state of sheer terror. We don't even get the chance to respond. While still laughing hard, they shrug their shoulders and disappear into the night. We are left floating in the air about 10 meters above the river.

"We'll see how to deal with them when we are through with the celebration." The purple figure trumpets this pronouncement as they fly out.

"No, we won't. In a few minutes, after the temperature drops a couple of degrees, they are all going to descend and free-fall towards the river." The yellowish courtesan woman spirited wording seems definitive.

"Then, their challenge is to find their internal power," observes the purple figure with a touting skeptical tone.
In the interim the six of us are literally paralyzed with fear.

"I can't move."

"Nothing to hang on to."

"Or grab either."

We all trumpet our dreaded anticipation.

"What do we do?" Breezie —the harlequin boy from China, asks everyone with a broken voice.

When I'm about to respond, all that can be heard are our screams of panic because suddenly we free-fall towards the river. When I'm about to hit the surface, I brace for the worst and close my eyes, but nothing happens. I don't feel the freezing water. I peek and there I am above the river standing on a thin layer of ice. I look around and see my five fellow harlequins standing alongside me with astonished faces like mine.

"Hey guys, now we can walk through fire and ice..." Reddish announces loudly remembering one of our powers.

"Let us walk slowly, cautiously, don't run." I warningly, say these words while we march with relieved faces towards the river's edge.

"Where are we going now?" Checkered wonders once we are all safely standing over dry land.

"Into the city to continue our search while our portal-power is back," Firee exclaims in a relieved voiced.

Hopping and jumping between buildings, using the spires as catapults, is fun, but the bumps, bruises, falls, and collisions are taking their toll. Yet we continue onward, doing so while running without a valid purpose under a menacing illuminated sky we've come to see, is a totally different, very risky, and dangerous proposition. Nevertheless, we must stay focused.

Across the city line we can see countless colorful spirits flying chaotically in all directions. They are causing mayhem throughout Prague, as they seemingly go unimpeded in and out of every corner, hook, and crack. We do our best to stay out of their way. They are so preoccupied with having fun at the expense of scaring and disturbing everyone that they don't notice us. After what feels like forever, we see the spirits return to the barges. Shortly afterwards, the faint sound of music precedes the continuation of the parade of barges as they journey on the river. The six of us are relieved to see them leave.

We peek down from a rooftop overlooking a small city square and a bright red dress catches our attention. We first see a small lady seated by the window of a Baroque designed five story building. Suddenly she vanishes.

We quickly scan across the way searching the square's balconies.

"There she is," Checkered, the harlequin girl from South-Africa, points to another balcony, not far from the first one.

Then she disappears again. Finally, after we've followed her disappearing act on and off, she seems to remain in one stationary place.

"She hasn't stopped staring at us," Checkered reports.

"How do you know?" Breezie asks.

"Look at her, she's gazing straight in our direction. Right now, I can even see her smiling," replies Checkered.

I do my best to inconspicuously observe this and in turn I realize that she is actually gesturing for us to come over. Passing through the building walls, the six of us approach her window and when we arrive, she hasn't moved standing in the same spot. We on the other hand have all transformed back to wearing our regular street clothes.

"Ah! The harlequins have arrived and much earlier than I expected." Hearing these mysterious words, we are led inside. "Our time clock unexpectedly leapt forward," says Checkered.

"I see, please come in," she announces as she opens a wide glass door.

We all stop at once when the red letters, painted at the entrance in a semi-circle, immediately hit us.

"Tetrikus Antique Writings for The Spirit and The Soul"
(Est. long, long time ago)

We enter the enormous facsimile of an amphitheater, decorated like an "old time" stage of another era with thick red velour curtains and an old wooden floor. Bookshelves are scattered everywhere.

"My name is Paulina Tetrikus, and I am the owner of this hallowed shop."

Then, we introduce ourselves one by one capturing her complete attention. She is short and hunched. For some reason she avoids looking at us straight in the eye. She has a beautiful and yet angry face. Her jet-black hair is closely cropped, and her green eyes appear stern.

'I'll bet she has a short fuse and a bad temper,' I guess while observing her.

"I've been monitoring your quest, so I have noticed a propensity amongst some of you to be envious of what others have versus what you do or don't have."

We all assent with our heads bobbing recognizing the presence of this attitude in our behavior.

"I have an ancient scribble that fits right into what we've been talking about. Let me read it to you. Appropriately, it is about the existential poison that is envy.

"The Three Bavarian Bakers"

Once upon a time
there were three bakers
in the town of Fürstenfeldbruck
near Munich
in the picturesque
southern German region of Bavaria.

Dieter, Kurt, and Helmut
were childhood friends
and had started baking at an early age
as their neighbor and idol, Has Neumann,
Dieter's father, was the best baker in town.

To their advantage,
he created all of his best recipes
and new creations
in secret at home in a separate building
his "Sanctum Sanctorum"
where he mixed and prepared
all his magic pastes.

His "baking-lab" was already stocked
with all the tools and ingredients he needed,
including a large oven
that constantly emanated
the magic scent of freshly baked treats.

Before or after school,
while he was at work at his lab,
the three curious kids would peek
at master baker Neumann when at work
and would run away when he noticed them.

But the sweet aroma
of all kinds of bread, pastries, tarts, and cakes
kept on drawing them back.

The busy baker was always aware of their presence,
but he let it be,
as he was not only bemused
by their enchanting childish games
but more importantly
because their persistence reassured him
of their genuine interest in his trade.

One good day when he felt they were ready for it,
he suddenly turned around
and staring intently in their direction
caught them by surprise
as the tightly bunched threesome
peeked through the window.

"There is no need for the three of you to hide."
Mr. Neumann said to the three eight years old
from his work bench.

"Come in, don't be shy."

The startled youngsters promptly complied
to his command.

Baker Neumann did not disappoint
as the three childhood friends
were promptly treated
with bites of the best tarts, cakes, and pastries
they'd ever eaten in their short lives.

At first, he sat them down to observe as he toiled.
As time went by,
he commenced explaining step by step
not only what baking was all about
but also how we was doing it.

He started to involve them
in the process
so, they learned to do it themselves.

Predicatively the three of them
went on to become bakers.

Kurt, became a master "baker,"
offering at his location,
more than a hundred different types
of freshly baked bread.

Helmut, became famous
as the best cake, tarts, and pies maker in the city,
ranging from wedding to coffee cakes.

Dieter became a "master confectioner"
offering the best pastries in town.

Unfortunately, their success also
marked the end of the friendship
between the three of them,
turning them into
fierce rivals and competitors.

"There is no better bread in Bavaria than yours Kurt,"
says Maria Schmidt, a regular customer,
she is referring
to the more than a hundred types of bread
on display at Kurt's famous bakery.

"The aroma of freshly baked bread,
there is none like yours,
hits me every time I'm near your place.
It simply pulls me in," adds Mrs. Schmidt.

"I agree there isn't better baker in South Germany.
I love your black bread,
soft and warm inside, crusty even hard on the outside.
A slice, spread with a natural marmalade
and a piece of Emmental cheese is heavenly for me,"
says Claudia Hoffbecker another of his loyal customers.

"Thank you, ladies,
your praise is definitely undeserved,"
Kurt replies politely.

But his mind is somewhere else.

'What good is it for me to be deemed the best baker in town
when the passion and profits of this business
can only be found in cakes and pastries,'
complains Kurt.

As usual,
the waiting line extends around the corner
of Helmut's Cake and Coffee Shop.

"Every few weeks on a Saturday
we drive all the way from Stuttgart
to enjoy Helmut's cakes. We love them,"
Brigitte Muller states passionately.

"We actually buy two or three at a time
so at home we can always have some.
But nothing compares to enjoying them here
warm, freshly made, just out of the oven,"
states Angela Schlushe to her close friend.

From his office window Helmut contemplates
his customers patiently standing in line.
His face though,
does not show either satisfaction or joy.

"What's the point of having so much loyalty and passion
come from my customers
if all the money is made on bread, pastries, and sweets."

Across town Ulrich enjoys a "Rote Grutze" dessert
with lots of white cream sauce,
Franz is delighted to taste the warm "ApfelStrudel"
blended in his mouth with Swiss vanilla ice cream.

"Hey Dieter, pastries craftsman,
what's up with your rivals
Kurt the bread maker and Helmut the cake maker?
Tell me, are they better than you?
Dieter's old friend Ulrich sternly asks
as he is now having a cappuccino.

"No, not at all, we are all masters at our own trade,"
Dieter replies.

"So, what's the problem then?" Interjects his friend, Franz.

"They both suffer from the same affliction.
They do not know how to enjoy their success.
Among other things,
they spend most of their time
not only criticizing what others do,

but even worst, comparing, and envying
what others have, and they don't.
As a result, they are never happy,"
Dieter reflects insightfully.

Mrs. Tetrikus shares her thoughtfulness once finished reading, "each of the childhood friends achieved success in their own right. They all enjoyed an enviable reputation, made high quality products, had economic success and yet only one of the three seemed to enjoy the achievements. The one that accepted his shortcomings —Dieter excelled at pastries but wasn't a good bread baker or cake maker —and yet he didn't envy what his friends had achieved or were good at doing. He was simply happy going about his trade without artificial poisons affecting his production." Mrs. Tetrikus views us with query eyes and a benevolent smile. "To learn to enjoy what you do and attain fulfillment at whatever you undertake, is the formula for happiness. On the other hand, envying others will guarantee your unhappiness with life." She has elaborated her understanding for us while she pulls out the familiar white envelope and hands it to me. It reads,

"Envy."

"Time for you to continue your quest before you run out of time." She says these words, and, in an instance, we are back at the same roof-top where we previously spotted her. Everyone gathers around me in expectation for now we have two unopened envelopes.

"It is best when they are opened in pairs," I reflect, recalling Thumbpee's words.

I open both envelopes and hand Generosity to Greenie and Envy to Checkered.

"The six antiquarians, along with their virtues and flaws, will be present as you attempt to cross the tunnel," reads Greenie.

An exalted Checkered follows. "Only the complete understanding of all you've learned will provide you with the necessary knowledge needed to overcome the obstacles you'll be facing."

The excitement of uncovering two more clues wears off rather quickly until, unexpectedly as his usual self, Thumbpee pops onto my shoulder. Being carefree he announces, "if your purpose is firm and clear, you'll be able to see through people's facades and perceive who they really are."

"Wow, another power! What is it? How do we use it?" I turn to ask Thumbpee but to no avail, he once more is gone.

"We have to go back," stresses Firee, the harlequin boy from India.

"Are we all in agreement on this?" I ask. "We don't want to make the same mistake," I warn, and everyone nods in agreement.

"Ok, where do we all want to go?" I ask. "The same place where we started," we all respond cohesively.

I swipe my hand in front of me, but nothing happens. One by one the others do so as well until Checkered's swipe causes our blurry portal to form in front of us. She steps in first and the rest of us rapidly follow. We step out and the brightness of midday in Prague hits us at once. We don't care. It feels great to return back in time, now with plenty of hours to spare to discover the answers required to succeed in our quest for qualify as wizard apprentices.

"Let's head to the square and confer again with The Orloj,"
I suggest without hesitating, and everyone marches along.

Chapter 6

"The Burly Man"

Standing in front of The Orloj there is no movement either from the sphere or the hands. None at all. The magnificent clock is inert, seemingly not alive!

"C'mon aspiring apprentices, join me over here," says the familiar voice.

Totally confused we all turn around chasing the source of the voice but come away with nothing.

"C'mon, all of you join me," repeats the burly man with the humongous mustache.

We walk towards the sound even more perplexed but as we get closer everything starts to make sense. The resemblance is uncanny and unmistakable.

"Are you…?" I start to ask the burly man.

"Of course, who else could I be," The Orloj announces puffing an immense Cuban cigar, "this is me when in daylight."

As we approach the human version of The Orloj, I notice right away that Thumbpee is back on my shoulder and Buggie's buzz has returned hovering directly above us.

"Orloj we've learned about the power of Humility and the perils of Pride. We've realized how fulfilling Generosity is and how unsavory a self-defeating Envy is," enunciates Firee, philosophically.

"I've been appraised of your progress and couldn't be more pleased, youngsters." The burly man acknowledges this while twirling his mustache incessantly.

"But we don't have the foggiest idea what any of the clues mean," says Reddish.

The Orloj contemplates the six of us, harlequins, with benign and bemused eyes.

"All in due time, all in due time. Be patient. Eventually it'll all make sense, most likely just before your final quest," preaches the spherical, time exacting mechanism.

Buggie's buzz suddenly intensifies and the batting of his wings becomes almost frantic. He starts to slowly fly away, as if prompting us to follow. Predictably, we all clumsily stumble while chasing after the tiny flying bugger.

"We'll be seeing you," I turn, shouting at The Orloj with apologetic eyes as I leave in a hurry.

"No worries, youngsters, go, go. I prefer meetings like this, short and sweet," declares the street version of the ancient clock.

"Where's Buggie heading?" Greenie feeling consternation inquisitively asks everyone as we are now trotting behind the noisy flying bug through Staromestske Namesti (Prague's Old Town Square).

"Why does that matter? Everything he's pointed out to us, has been not only accurate but has resulted in either a statue, a shop, a virtue, a flaw, or the corresponding clues," Reddish negates her concern.

Ahead of us, at the far end of the mammoth square, a small crowd has gathered. Buggie's prying tiny green laser is pointed at the back of a tall, statuesque woman with blond hair bundled in a ponytail; she's part of a group of street performers playing a small piano, a colorful accordion, a trumpet and she is on the violin. The quartet plays tunes that at times seem to be Blues, Jazz, and other melodies right off the streets of Montmartre, the bohemian's, and artist's quarters in Paris.

Half of the spectators are standing in various poses, the rest float in the air. The peculiar crowd's clothes are eccentric exhibiting every color combination there is in the spectrum of light. The performers outfits are shiny and sparkling, as literally accompanying every high note, little stars and lightning bolts jump out of them to the delight of the spectators.

"You guys want to join the show?" A medium sized heavily mustached and eye-browed man wearing a top hat, dressed like an early 1900s' mortician approaches us.

'He's a bit intimidating,' I think to myself.

"Yes, we would, why not?" The six of us bunch-up with the sole purpose of not taking our eyes off the tall, bony blond woman playing the violin.

As we join the crowd, I start to feel uncomfortable, I notice a number of men, all with the same menacing appearance similar to the mortician look alike, starting to close in and surround us. He is the leader of the pack.

Then it happens. With a deft hand-gesture, almost like a military salute, conducted by each of them circling us, the arms of the six of us harlequins, are involuntarily hoisted straight up. A hands-in-the-air feat, driven by magic. Then in rapid succession, as they approach us, our legs are lifted-up as well. It is an awkward position imitating clothes hanging to dry that we find ourselves in. That's when Greenie, the harlequin girl from Lebanon, sees them for what they really are.

"These men are not who they pretend to be," says Greenie in a rush of words.

'She is unknowingly, using one of the powers we've just acquired,' I realize. Then, it suddenly hits me. 'With a clear purpose we may become...'

And that's how, for the first time, we, aspiring wizard apprentices become invisible to others. Great timing, especially for the astonished bunch around us. Now standing up, I lead the other five with a finger covering my mouth to indicate silence. Invisibly, we all pass unnoticed through the menacing pack.

"They are gargoyles," Greenie reveals, and we are all now fully aware of this, thanks to our new power that enables us to see people for what they really are.

The tall blond woman is packing her instrument and leaving, so we follow her through the streets of Prague. She carries her precious violin as if it were her child. At that moment we realize that we are dressed again in our everyday clothes.

'She can't see us. We are invisible. No one can see us, but we can see one another. Wow! I'm flabbergasted.'

Chapter 7

"Time to Decide"

Did she just morph into an old lady holding a cane?" Asks a bewildered Breezie.

We all see Buggie's validating miniscule green laser, pointing at her. Remaining invisible, we all nod affirmatively and simply follow shadowing her closely.

Now her violin is being wheeled about in a shopping cart. She seems to be walking straight into a cobble-stone wall, but just short of reaching it, she swipes her hand, and a tunnel materializes. She quickly walks through, and we follow several steps after. The pursued, and we, the pursuers, exit the tunnel only to find ourselves at a city park.

"Amazing, what a short cut," acknowledges Reddish.

Morphing into her original persona, the tall blond woman rents a rowboat and quickly paddles away. We the invisible bunch trot around the small lake without taking our eyes off her until we safely reach the other end where she seems to be heading. She disembarks from the boat and walks a few steps to an underpass which crosses over the parks' main road. She stops right in the middle of it, turns to face the side wall, swipes her hand again and walks right into an opening, through a narrow passage that appears on the solid wall. The six of us promptly follow, then the opening disappears behind our backs. We see the Stars of David on the tombstones and quickly realize that we are in Prague's Jewish Cemetery. Returning to her original appearance, the tall blond lady quickens her pace walking through the entire cemetery, reaching the back of it in a whisk. Adjacent on the border outside, we see for the first time, a three-story building with a huge, mounted hand-painted sign that reads,

"Dillettante and Dillettante Antiquarians" (Est. a century and half ago)

"This is the only way to arrive here." The tall lady loudly announces these words, with her back facing us, as she opens the door.

We don't know how to respond but assume she cannot be talking to anyone else but us.

The statuesque woman slowly turns around and properly facing the group, connects with each one of us by directly boring into each one of our eyes. Instantly, we all become visible.

"Did you think for a moment that I didn't know, or should I say, that I did not see you, as you were following me. Aspiring apprentices, your powers of invisibility do not work on the statues," she reveals as she enters motioning for us to do the same. We enter and are immediately struck by the three-story high atrium directly in the center of the magnificent building. The bookshelves are of similar height.

"Aspiring apprentices, please be seated." she indicates where, pointing to a large sofa at the atrium's center.

After serving us lemonade and cookies, she gets straight to the point.

"One of the key virtues you must develop or discover within yourselves and foster in pursuing a fulfilling life is compassion. When we show sympathy and sorrow for the misfortunes of others and when we act to help or assist to diminish hardships or do away with them, we are showing compassion. I'm going to attempt to illustrate this virtue with a timeless reading. Please allow me…"

Next, Mrs. Dilettante with all of the splendor of her Scandinavian roots in play, earnestly starts to read:

"The Wounded Tiger"

He hides between the green and yellow leaves,
his muscular and massive body perfectly blended
high-above the branches of the majestic tree,
one of only a handful around
as the bush's grounds look scorched
by the intense heat.

The powerful muscular beast in hiding
lays in wait ready to attack.
He is restless, impatient, and overly thirsty,
his mouth and throat are utterly dry.

But he is hungry and that clouds his instincts.
At this moment, his sole focus of attention
is on a young gazelle, playing in the vicinity,
separated from the herd
unwittingly getting closer and closer
to the tiger's killer zone.

Unbeknownst to the hunting tiger
he is about to be hunted as well.
The two rifle men have him in their sights
with their long-range weapons
aiming straight at him.

Then, both actions happen simultaneously,
the tiger moves ever so slightly ready to jump,
the shooters fire at the same time.
Both shots miss and the tiger takes off
in full knowledge that he is running for his life.

While the panicking tiger scuds away,
his speed is frantic, chaotic, and precipitous.

The shooters manage to get two more rounds off
when the beautiful animal is almost out of range.
One shot misses, the second only grazes his back.

But although causing a slight stumble,
it does not slow him down,
and a split second later, he is gone.

Eventually, at last,
after a seemingly endless run,
the wounded tiger makes his way back to the pack.

He lays down and right after a few pants and moans,
passes out, while a trickle of bright red blood
slowly makes its half-way through his torso and into his legs.

A couple of females approach him
and start licking his wound,
a band of youngsters does the same
but only the little cubs can reach
his blood-stained legs with their tongues,
they eagerly lick the tasty red liquid.

"Maybe this time, we'll get rid of him for good."

"I sincerely hope your wishes come true."

"I am sick and tired of this super-hero among us."

"Perhaps we should all move and get out of here."

"The hunters may still be chasing him."

"And abandon him here?"

"Who cares? He may not make it anyhow."

"It is quite dark already. They will be gone by now,
too dangerous in the dark for them
as they can easily become the hunted,
besides, we don't leave any of us behind."

Suddenly,
a small commotion of grunts
signals something abnormal.
A couple of tigers from another pack
hesitantly approach the wounded tiger.

Everyone is alert and tense,
ready to fight.
But the marauding tigers are not
in an attacking mode.

They slightly bump the females over to the side,

and they all stand aside albeit reluctantly
although remaining close by.

The visitors start to lick the wound intensely,
even appearing to suck out the wound's blood.

Next, one of the visiting tigers
brushes his paw with a white chalk
for a split second
over the wound
and shortly thereafter, they are gone.

The following morning the tiger wakes up
and starts to walk gingerly around,
his wound on the mend,
he is getting ready to soon go hunting
once again.

"See, young harlequins, compassion is not only the thought but the action."

"I didn't think I had much compassion in me 'till now." Checkered shares her thoughts while the rest of us nod acknowledging a collective attitude.

"What I've been taught, since I was a child, over and over again is to avoid the weak, otherwise they'll drag me down alongside them. Incorrectly, I thought that the strong always straddled the strong discarded the weak believing that in life one should never be weak and keep distance from this as well."

"And what have you guys learned today?" Mrs. Dilettante asks.

"That there is nothing wrong with helping and caring for the weak," I reply.

"It is actually a moral obligation to identify other's misfortunes and if possible, helpfully act on them as well," the antiquarian affirms.

"Congratulations!" She responds, while focusing on us, her eyes benign and pleased. Next, the antiquarian swipes her hand in slow motion. And just like that, both she and her spot vanish, and we once again are standing in the middle of the Jewish cemetery.

"Look," Reddish, the harlequin girl from Spain, says while pointing at the white envelope I am holding.

"Open it Blunt," says Breezie and I do so reading aloud:

"Compassion."

"But isn't it better to open the envelopes in pairs?" Reddish interrupts hesitatingly.

"Now that times is off the essence and given our progress so far, we should take our chances and proceed to open this one." I assert.

"We are about to complete the quest, we need to know what's ahead of us," asserts Firee.

Everyone nods. So, I open it and read it aloud.

"Even though time will be pressing and constrained, you must ignore it completely. In order to succeed, you'll need to act outside of the constraints of time even as the clock continues to tick and tick away.

We all look at each other and are as clueless and confused as ever. Ignore time while it is running out, what a paradox! I believe the answer will become evident. We must continue to believe and move forward. After a while I shrug my shoulders and lead the others out of the cemetery. Almost predictably, my conscience in this parallel world, once again pops-up, sitting on top of my shoulder with one leg crossed.

"You'll have the power to read what is in the mind of others as long as you don't reveal it to your target," announces trusty Thumbpee. When I turn around to ask him a pointed question, the Lilliputian is already gone.

"Let's get out of here guys, we still have one more statue to find."

Chapter 8

"Never Enough"

Back in our harlequin clothes, our small band strolls through the mysterious streets that comprise the wicked city. The place is bewitched bustling with all kinds of activities conjured by the sorcerers with their incantations. It is not so much the flying broomsticks or the driven explosions but rather the noises and swooshes that are captivating. There is also the creepy and unexpected including the occasional Jokers' strident and continuous laughter, and their usual contemptuous behavior. Thumbpee is all of a sudden back again resting on top of one of my shoulders.

Slightly ahead of me, Reddish is standing in front of a narrow dead-end street. She seems to be in a trance as we join her. A faint melody can be heard from afar. The five of us all turn around and look in the same direction that she is fixated on and are quickly as taken as she is. A small gathering of fifty or so people are watching a band of four perform.

"Three of the four artists are the same street musicians we saw earlier at the square," Checkered notes.

"But Mrs. Dilettante has been replaced with a red hair, roundish man who is playing the bass," observes Reddish.

"I wonder why?" Point Reddish.

However, the guy that catches our attention is not a band member, but instead a spectator like us. He is a bundle of fidgeting nerves and cannot stay still. He has puffy eyes, his clothes are hanging, is sickly skinny, of average height with a mat of wrangled chestnut curled hair. He nonstop mumbles to himself. He breaks away and just out of a gut feeling, I decide to follow him with my other fellow harlequins tagging along.

"Where did he go?" Checkered wonders as immediately turning left leading the way into a small alley, we lose sight of him.

"Youngsters, youngsters come over here," are the happy words we hear from behind our backs.

Turning around as one, we see standing under a broken streetlamp, a big middle-aged woman, wearing a deep blue and white, long colorful skirt with matching long sleeves and head scarf; and has cascades of flowing jet-black hair and intense caramel eyes. She is playing the harmonica while a half-asleep dog whales in sync to her tune and a small monkey wearing a tiny round circus hat, stands winding the handle of a music box while he moves with the music. It rhymes to perfection with the melody she performs. We watch and listen to the music for what seems to be an eternity.

"What do you think, is she the missing guy?" I ask Reddish.

"You mean the curled hair bony man we were following?"

"Mm," I mumble.

"No, she is she."

"Fine then, let's go."

"Wait, wait, don't leave yet. I've got something of value for you," implores the old lady.

We stop and watch her closely, wearing totally baffled faces. But otherwise, we say nothing.

"I've a got a proposition for you," she offers.

We remain motionless and speechless.

"I will trade a cheat-sheet on how to cross the tunnel to the castle; additionally, I can trade the answers to the final test you'll have to successfully complete in the castle's tunnel, in order to earn your credentials as wizard apprentices."

"In exchange for what?" We all ask.

"Your powers and clues."

'Tempting but fishy,' thinks Reddish as we communicate silently by using our powers.

'We are alertly listening to your thoughts,' I think this, and everyone hears me except the peculiar lady.

'I say we do it,' thinks Breezie picking up the momentum.

'What about if it is just a ruse?' We wonder.

'No pain, no gain. If we don't take risks, how can we succeed? I say we take a vote right now,' Breezie thinks this while pushing for the go-ahead decision. 'Wait a minute guys, there's something that doesn't add up in this scenario. If she supposedly has a solution about how to cross the tunnel, she doesn't need the clues we hold or the powers we have acquired.'

'So, it is a trick,' I conclude.

'Probably,' we all surmise this probability at once in our common thinking. 'Reddish using your powers, check if she is a witch and what she is thinking right now.'

'Ok,' she transmits while focusing on the middle-aged lady.

'Guys, you're not going to believe this, but what she's thinking is not really originating from her, but from a third party that is giving her instructions directing what to say.

At that moment the middle-aged lady blinks as if to refocus, seemingly with benign and loving eyes while she continues to play her music, ignoring the offer she just made to us. We see the sign that is disguised under her long hair.

'She's blind,' communicates a surprised Reddish.

'Aspiring wizard apprentices,' is the loud voice that fills the air.

As our costumes transform back to our street clothes, we see the man we were following earlier.

"I'm Morpheus Rubicom. It was me speaking through her," he announces with a thunderous voice. "I've just tested your avarice inclination and you've all passed with flying colors. Congratulations!"

You were close to succumbing to temptation by pursuing the easy way out but ultimately withstood the impulse through collective effort and good judgment. Always remember, avarice can without intent take hold and blindside you at any time. What we chase if infected by this poison is fool's gold," he continues. "You couldn't detect the lie because the old lady was not lying. It was me who was deceptive. It wasn't until you penetrated what she was really thinking that allowed you to detect that it wasn't her own thoughts but rather mine," he expands.

"Come with me, let's go to the shop."

Less than half a block later, with a couple of gargoyles flanking it, we see the sign.

"Rubicom Antiquarians, Books about Wealth, Fame and Love"
(est. several generations ago)

"Don't mind them, these two are at my service," he says easing our apprehension caused by the evil escort.

Somewhat uncomfortable, we step into what is a very small space, having a low ceiling, saturated wall to wall with books.

"My specialty is home delivery. Very seldom do I get visitors here," Rubicom explains to us as if reading our minds.

"Squeeze yourselves into that bench," he tells us with a matter-of-fact tone, that there, in no other available spot. Once all of us somehow are seated, he continues. "Youngsters, on the subject of avarice, I have a timeless tale that sums up the whole concept very well.

"The Gold Men from Cuzco"

Julio Velazco-Piana and Ramón Ernesto Soto-Duarte
bought and sold gold for a living.

Their shops competed fiercely.
Both rivals were strategically located
high-up the Andean mountain range
at the touristic small town of Cuzco,
Peru's getaway to Machu-Pichu,
the fabled ancient remains
of a city that was once at the heart
of the Inca civilization.

Julio's trade was booming.
Over time he had been deft
at securing multiple and many sources for his gold.

He promptly paid the best price in the market
for what was offered to him.

Hence, almost every gold seller in the region
countless individuals and businesses,
legitimate or not,
went to him.

In addition, he was a master trainer of his trade,
with these skills he built in just a few years,

the best and most talented stable
of gold handcrafters,
all of it resulting in gold jewelry
that was by far the highest quality
available in the mountains region,
if not perhaps the country.

Peruvian and foreign tourists
loved his shop,
buyers from all sorts of life and
places came to him to buy his gold
products.

Ramón Ernesto on the other hand
was much more modest
in his practice and aspirations,
so, he bought less and paid more for the
gold, resulting in a significantly smaller
offering of gold products,
all of it resulting in sales
that were easily ten times less
than his competitor, Julio's operations.

Despite this the quality of both
their jewels and ornaments
were pretty similar.

But when profits were accounted for,
Ramón Ernesto,
with a significantly smaller and less famous place,
made significantly more money than Julio.

Simply by being a lot smaller

and having fewer expenses
even if the gold cost him more,
it cost Ramón Ernesto significantly less
to manufacture each piece of jewelry.

Further,
when hard times fell on the country,
and was accompanied by a steep sales drop
Julio had to downsize in a hurry,
otherwise he could have gone bust.

Hence the paradox of avarice.
He who covets without limit or moderation,
always loses in the long run
to the one not possessed by avarice.

Rubicom lectures insightfully and wisely, "young aspiring apprentices, you have successfully completed your quest. Here is your card. Now let me get you guys some refreshments and pastries. You deserve and have earned them."

Breezie receives the envelope, and it reads:

"Avarice"

He immediately tears it open and reads aloud.

"The dangers that are ahead of you, as you move through the tunnel, will test your good judgment and calm while under pressure, a challenging exercise to utilize all that you've learned."

"At least this is understandable," I declare.

Soon we are all back in our harlequin clothes. We are all seated in an exhausted condition and are eager to lay back and enjoy Mr. Rubicom's treats. Minutes go by, soon half an hour. We call him persistently, but to no avail.

"He's not coming guys," I say in resignation.

"Then why we are all still here, the place has not vanished," observes Firee.

"Only its owner is gone," points out Reddish with her typical sarcasm.

"Guys, remember the first clue?" reminds Greenie.

"The tunnel's door lies underneath the old scribble."

We all turn and look at the book Mr. Rubicom has just read to us. Greenie instinctively pushes the book to the side. The moment she slides it ever so slightly, a shrill chirring noise echoes throughout the store. A bit louder and the sound becomes unbearable.

"Move it all at once," I rapidly command.

And so, it happens. Once the book is completely moved to the side, the noise stops. Ahead of us, replacing an entire side of the tiny bookstore is a cave with a totally dark entrance.

"What is this?" Asks Reddish. "Wait a minute, is that the…? Recognition registers with the coterie. "Yes! Finally, the entrance to the Castle's tunnel."

Chapter 9

"Reckoning"

"The Humility Challenge"

With trepidation, we all step into the cavern. The surface is wet and feels slippery. Unexpectedly, we are back in our street clothes, which means that imminent trouble lurks ahead. Water continues to trickle down from above and soon we are paralyzed with fear, unable to proceed. The first to lose footing is me, followed almost simultaneously by the other five. The hard surface is not only smooth like glass, but slightly inclined. Stumbling and sliding on our backs along the wet surface, we start to gather speed and our expressions of angst turn into muffled cries. The surface is progressively more and more inclined, so we pick-up even more momentum. Now our voices turn to screams.

"We've got to use our powers!" I yell.

"Which one? I can't figure out the one that will work," Breezie snaps back.

"Our powers do not work in here."

But the conversation is interrupted by the drop-off. The surface now turns into a wet bowl, where we zoom down and around still screaming in terror. Suddenly the drop-off ends abruptly, and we are thrown into the air only to lunge straight down into a subterranean pool of deep water. The moment we surface, I reply to Breezie:

"I can't figure any way out," I barely enunciate this words as the strong current drags us into a narrow passage that is formed like a cone.

The water compression through the smaller passage accelerates our speed. As soon as we enter, the tube turns into the curves of a spiral. We start spinning around in circles and now our frantic yelps can be heard. But all to no avail. There is no one in here to help us. The sudden jump knocks the air out of my lungs. Same for the others. We land back in the water tube, and right away another jump-off follows. The situation, as we gather even more speed, is quickly turning life threatening.

"What do we do to make us stop? Help!" Yells Reddish.

Another drop-off sends us into the void but this time we are in the air longer and flying further, so we hit the water with a smack. It knocks us out of our senses.

"Got it, got it, let's show humility guys," screams an out of breath Checkered.

"How?" Cries out Greenie with a drained sound exhaling from her voice.

"Let's try this. We simply don't know. We have no clue indicating how to resolve this situation. Please help us!"

Abruptly, we are standing in the tunnel, and are totally dry and back in our harlequin outfits.

"Youngsters, well done, proud of you, above all you've displayed profound humility during the direst of circumstances. Good luck on the rest of your journey," says Cornelius Tetragor, the tall man with the massively long beard and robe as he ever so briefly steps out of the tunnel shadows. He nods his head and smiles effusively from ear to ear.

"Sir, what comes next..." I'm not able to complete my words as the bearded man is gone faster than he arrived."

"Through the trickling river, past your worst fears," I recite. "That's what the rest of the first clue read," I say recalling and thinking aloud.

"That was some kind of trickling river," says Reddish broadcasting Iberian sarcasm.

"The Pride Test"

We have barely taken a few steps in the tunnel, when I see a tiny, teeny yellow dot in front of me. It moves along responding to my body gestures. I try to grab it, but it reacts too quickly.

"Blunt, what is with this light following me?" Asks Firee.

"Me as well," blurts Greenie.

When I look around, I can see that we all have a point of light in front of us.

"Look, it is jumping with me," says Breezie.

"As I swing my head, the light is doing the same," I observe.

"Can you all see the black dot in it? It looks like an eye, and I feel like I'm being watched," says Checkered.

"You mean us," says Reddish.

"Spooky," babbles Breezie.

"Hey guys, I've got two now," announces Firee.

"Me too," follows Checkered.

"I've got a third," timidly adds Reddish.

Like popcorn, the light specs start to multiply at an astonishing rate and pace. Pretty soon, we are surrounded by thousands of them. That's when they start to close ranks.

"They are getting closer to me, I don't like this one bit," says a very nervous sounding Greenie.

"Guyyys, they are lifting me up," says Breezie with a voice filled with wonder.

Instantly we are all floating in the air if we were lying on our beds with thousands upon thousands of tiny lights bunched together serving as our mattresses. Back in our street clothes, we are all weary as if sensing a certain imminent danger that we are unable to figure out. That's when things turn wild. I am thrown violently sideways into the air by my mattress made out of thousands of tiny lights. I head at full speed, headfirst, towards the rocky walls of the tunnel. Everyone else as well is thrown randomly in different directions. I brace myself anticipating impact but just before it happens, I bounce back off a wall of lights that forms in front of the hard concrete wall. In rapid succession, they begin to recklessly throw and catch me in the same fashion, just preventing a crash. The same is happening to the others as well. Next, I am suspended in the air, head pointing down, feet up just being held by one of my feet.

Then, they begin to move me sideways, and the others are quickly in the same position. Now I face what appears to be a bottomless pit. Before I have time to react, they toss me into the void. The effect of my screams as I fall is exponentially enhanced by the echoes of the narrow walls. These annoying lights are following me on my way down.

'Are they giggling?' I wonder feeling vibrating and disturbing fear. 'No, they are forming a phrase,' I realize as the words begin to form.

"Underneath, pointed arrows await you...also fiery flames...like it?...Hahaha!..."

The wind speed hurts my face and makes it very difficult to adjust my eyes and view what's underneath, but slowly through the darkness I see tiny flickers appearing in the distance. 'What do we have left, just a few seconds to live?' I ask myself in despair.

I can hear the despairing screams of the other five, surely in the same predicament, dropping to their deaths. Strangely my thinking becomes clearer by the second, in a way I can't understand. Time seems to slow down and the same seems to be happening to the others. I am hazily sensing our shared circumstance.

'What do we do Blunt?' Breezie surprises me out of the blue with his thoughts penetrating my head.

'How is this happening?' I ask.

'We are learning to handle stress and pressure,' just at the right moment realizes Firee. Her instincts are so accurate.

'I know, guys, I know, I've got it!' Announces Checkered bursting with emotion.

'Well, you better hurry because those lights underneath are approaching fast,' cautions the ever-nervous Greenie.

'We swallow our pride and concede that we cannot solve this problem without the statues' help,' continues Checkered.

'Statues we need your assistance to figure a way out of this situation,' she pleads.

And in a snap, although at a different section, we are all back, standing in the tunnel with no sign of the mischievous lights around. We hear an emanating voice.

"Youngsters, in life sometimes all we need to do is to put our pride aside and simply ask for help. That's what you have just done. Congratulations!" Says Lazarus Zeetrikus, the tall old man with the bent top hat, who welcomes us with a big broad smile.

This time we don't even try to respond and predictably he's gone, puff, in an instant. Now again we are back in our harlequin clothes. Looking at each other, we know that we have to move forward. Unexpectedly, Reddish assumes the initiative on her own, encompassing an exuberant Latin passion approach.

"Come on you all, let me give you guys a big hug," she insists, and we all embrace in a gigantic pile-on.

Some cry in relief, others laugh but what we all are is totally relaxed and joyful. Somehow the stress is gone.

"The dangers awaiting you as you move through the tunnel under pressure will test your good judgment and calm under pressure. This exercise is a test of all you've learned." I recall voicing these words aloud as another of the clues with the agreement and consensus of the group members.

"Time to proceed," I assert bringing everyone back to reality,

"The Gratitude Test"

Two abreast we walk along the narrow path for about a hundred yards until something strange happens. Absolute silence engulfs us. We can't even hear our own footsteps, much less our voices. The place falls into absolute silence. In the dim lights of the tunnel, we all draw puzzled expressions. Then, back again to our street clothes, we hear a faint tick, but nothing else. As we move forward a few more steps, the tick becomes many ticks. Further ahead is an army of ticks, encroaching even closer until it becomes an overwhelming roar of ticks. That's when we see them. Thousands of clocks. Wall mounted, free standing, round, square, rectangular, roman numeral, without numbers, only bars, all of them ticking. The sound is deafening. Suddenly, we are all separated from one another as semicircles of time measuring devices form around each of us. I'm surrounded by countless clocks. The intense light emanating out of them at first blinds me, but as my eyes adjust, I see that each one has a tiny video screen. As I look closer, the realization hits me like a thunderbolt. Each screen shows images from different moments in my life. They are moving at high speed, so at first, it's very difficult for me to appreciate the visual memories as they appear in front of me. Instinctively, I try to slow down the hand of one of the clocks and it responds! One move and voilà! All images in the tiny screens of every clock are adjusted as well. "The minutes" longer hands, respond best when observing the small details of life's passages, "The hours" shorter hands, are perfect for slowing down the complete picture and overviews of my entire life's chapters. I see my aunties and uncles, my much younger adoptive parents, I gaze at the mischief and tantrums that I had. Then I freeze the images of my deceased biological parents when they come into view. When I see myself being born, tears start to cascade down my face. I shiver with emotion seeing how much they loved one another. Both so young, my father looking strong, handsome, my mom ethereally beautiful. Time flies, and the last image I manage to watch, is one I will never forget. Both my parents are waving goodbye and blowing a kiss to me, their baby. For the moment it feels as if their gesture is directed at me now, in the present.

"Thank you very much," I, in rhapsody, shout. "However, this has taken place, whoever did this, it has been amazingly wonderful!" I continue with a teary voice.

Without any indication or warning, we find ourselves back in the tunnel. An empty path is ahead of us. We look at each other painstakingly dazed and we realize from the emotion in all of our faces, that we've all partaken in similar experiences.

"Harlequins, you've just experienced life's clock ticking away, and you were gifted with wonderful moments in time past, now earned through your perseverance, dedication, and open mindedness. You've all displayed impeccable decorum by expressing profound gratitude for the key memories you were able to experience, which always is the best reward for one's generosity. Each of you for the first time witnessed crucial moments in your life. All six of you immediately reacted graciously, in a thankful, appreciative manner for what was given to you. Congratulations!" Says Lucrecia Van Egmond, the impossibly tall middle-aged lady with long threaded white hair, fine gestures, pale skin, aquiline nose, milky blue eyes and wearing an ankle long skirt with matching long sleeves and scarf. "You are well on your way to your goal, but do not become complacent, there are still plenty of dangers and risks ahead of you." She says all this and vanishes in an instant.

As we walk further down the tunnel, I recall another of the clues.

"Even though time is pressing and constrained, you'll have to ignore it completely. In order to succeed you'll need to act outside the restraints of life's clock as it ticks and ticks away."

Suddenly we realize that we are back to our harlequin clothes.

"The Envy Test"

As soon as we start walking, we hear voices in the distance. The sounds are animated, seemingly in high spirits. We then see the six shadows and immediately register that they are children our age. When their images come into focus, what we see are six harlequins wearing broad smiles on their faces, as they grin from ear to ear.

"Oh, aspiring wizard apprentices," the tallest, a boy says in a mocking tone.

Teases a red-haired young girl, "we've graduated already!"

'How I wish to be them,' I mutter for a moment.

A green harlequin with eyes of the same color asks us, "do you want us to give you some tips, maybe some hints to complete your quest?"

We all look at each other and shrug our shoulders, uncertain of our answer.

"Why n…" I begin to reply in consent but interrupt myself halfway through.

"Wait a minute guys, perhaps we shouldn't, wouldn't that be cheating?" I point out aloud.

"You must be the leader," the tallest of the graduates inquires.

"Call me Blunt."

"I'm Hawk. Wouldn't you like to be like us, a fully accredited wizard apprentice?"

"Of course, but..."

"Blunt, now I recall The Orloj saying that we must cross the tunnel on our own without interference," raises Reddish.

"Hey, wait a minute, I recall something else," adds Greenie jumping in.

"There's is only one group of aspiring wizard apprentices at any one time chasing the credentials."

We all turn around and look at the other harlequin band. Their expressions have just changed to disgust and anger before they vanish.

"Gargoyles," we all say as one.

"And we couldn't detect them because our powers don't work down here," says Firee.

"How could they? We are walking under the river Vltava," adds Breezie.

"Bravo!" Are the words of the familiar and beautiful voice stepping out of the tunnel shadows. Here's Paulina Tetrikus, short and hunched with a short fuse of a temper; a beautiful but angry face that rarely looks straight at anyone's eyes. Today though she's obviously abandoning her usual persona and comfort zone since she's wearing an immense smile of satisfaction while staring at each one of us without even a blink.

"That's how envy is stifled, by pausing, weighing, and thinking, instead of coveting what others can do or have but we don't. We do this by gratefully focusing on what we possess without losing sight of the task at hand," she says in animated spirits. "I just loved the team effort," are her last words before she disappears in a swoosh of dust and smoke.

"The six antiquarians, along with the virtues and flaws will be present as you attempt to cross the tunnel." I recall aloud one more of the clues. The others assent with their heads shaking in total understanding that through our quest all of the clues are coming to fruition. Right at that moment, our clothes revert to harlequin outfits.

"The Test of Avarice"

As we turn a corner, the tunnel bifurcates in two directions. Promptly, we split into two groups.

"Guys, whatever you find or come across, do not face it by yourselves. We will all return to this point to decide our strategy before there is any interaction."

Reddish, Breezie, and I walk through a passage that becomes narrower and narrower as we move forward, continuing until we cannot go any further.

"This is definitely not the way!" Breezie declares so we turn back.

But as we leave, I keep looking back over my shoulder while thinking that perhaps we didn't search the area sufficiently. When we reach the intersection, we find that Greenie, Checkered and Firee are all jumping up and down celebrating something.

"We found it, we found it!" Greenie announces.

"Found what?"

"The castle. The exit to it is right there, at the end of this passage. We were about to walk out when we remembered your words."

Excited, the six of us walk towards the end of the tunnel and to our surprise our harlequin clothes are back on. This makes us pause. Firee is guiding us as he has already been to the site. We contemplate reaching the castle at the other end, but all of the sudden he slows down way before we are able to even see the exit.

"Guys, we've not completed the six tests or challenges pertaining to the virtues and flaws," he brings up disappointedly.

"So, maybe this is a shortcut, perhaps our reward for doing so well. What are we waiting for? Let's go, c'mon we should be running," says Reddish, without too much conviction in her voice.

"We can't." I say.

All five turn around and look at me, with surprised but expectant faces because of the seriousness of my words.

"In order to complete passage through the tunnel, we'll have to deal with all the virtues and flaws first." I recall this, resonating the words imparted to us at the beginning of our quest. "That's what The Orloj said at our first encounter." I add, "besides we are back in our harlequin clothes, that clearly tells us that this is not the way."

"So, what do we do now?" Asks Firee.

"We turn around and return to the tunnel intersection." And that's what we do, but to our surprise the intersection has disappeared and there is no way forward.

"You'll all be master wizards one day," these surprising words come from somewhere within the tunnel. "The behavior you've displayed just now, demonstrates mature behavior well beyond your years. You could have easily sought instant gratification, and you could have succumbed to wanting more than you needed. But instead of surrendering your resolve, you resisted temptation and did away with avarice, keeping your eye on the task at hand."

These words come from Morpheus Rubicom, the tall man with the loose hanging clothes. Today his usual nervousness and puffy eyes are almost imperceptible, replaced by his jubilant mood, though his incessant movement continues. Then he vanishes and we are all left with a sense of satisfaction but light angst for what could have been.

"Only the complete knowledge of what you've learned along the way, will provide you with the required wisdom to overcome the obstacles you'll be facing," I recite aloud one more of the clues.

"Those were great instincts, I mean, that we exhibited," a philosophical Reddish responds.

"And proficient. We've learned a lot on this journey," I add complementing her words.

Our harlequin clothes are back once again.

"The Compassion Challenge"

We take the longest walk since we started our journey. Streetlamps now light the way, giving us a sense of proximity. All of a sudden out of nowhere, an intense sulfur smell affects us. It is followed by an intense red aura that filters through the air. We enter an immense chamber that looks more like a cave. Our street clothes are back. Right in front of us, we face an abyss that definitely cannot be crossed without aid. Sulfur red fumes emanate up from the bottomless hole. From the other end of the abyss, we hear a metallic sound. A retractable narrow bridge starts to extend toward us from the other side. It has the shape of a horizontal fire truck ladder.

"Youngsters, you're almost there," proclaims Lettizia Dillettante the antiquarian Nordic beauty with blond hair that is pulled back into a ponytail. Self-aware but humble, her expression is one of absolute self-confidence.

A click sounds as the bridge automatically reaches us, locking its latches to the ground, providing us with confidence that we inherently are completing the quest.

"Harlequins, there is one final virt..." her words are interrupted by a massive tremor that shakes the entire chamber. The ground starts to crumble, rock debris fall from above as the red sulfur fumes filter upward through brand new forming cracks. All of us struggle to maintain balance but keep a safe distance away from the precipice's edge. But no sooner than we respite, a second tremor follows this time much stronger. The entire place seems ready to collapse. Worst of all, the trembling does not stop. We can see the bridge swaying from side to side, seemingly about to fail or fall. Finally, to our great relief, when the tremor ends, we hear the latches unlock, signaling that the bridge is going to retract.

"Where's Mrs. Dillettante?" asks Reddish.

The bridge is about to move! We all step on it so the retraction immediately stops. That's when I see her, facing the abyss, her back against the wall, standing on a precarious ledge of the abyss wall, ten feet below the surface level.

"I'm going to help her. Breezie come with me. The rest of you start to cross the bridge, we'll see you on the other side." I am rapid firing the words.

But the moment I step-off the bridge, it starts to retract. I quickly step back on, and the retraction stops.

"Blunt, it requires that all six of us stand on it otherwise it retracts," says Firee.

"Then, we all step down, we can't leave her isolated over there." I say this and everyone agrees immediately.

We all quickly get off and head towards her. The roar wells up from the ground once more and it begins to tremble with increasing intensity. The bridge is still there but none of us look back. Then, we hear the metallic sound of the ladder latches disengaging and know that our opportunity to cross over the abyss to reach the other side, is gone. We reach the ground's edge. She's right underneath inside the hole, hanging by a thread and ready to be swallowed by the abyss' jaws. I extend a hand to her while two others hold me. Breezie does the same getting a hold of her other hand. The ground now starts to rupture around us. In the meantime, the bridge is halfway back as it retracts to the other side. The tremors increase in earnest! We struggle not to lose balance, but when Breezie and I try to pull the antiquarian up, we fail! We don't have the combined strength to lift her weight.

"C'mon Blunt, Breezie, together you can do it." Reddish urges us on with tears of concern coating her eyes.

"She is slipping away. We are losing her," I reactively shout out of frustration.

Then the ledge crumbles under her feet. We close our eyes waiting for the straining tug to happen, yet we don't let go of her hands. Hoping for the impossible, we anticipate the pull that will either release her when we lose our grip or pull us down with her. Astonishingly, it never happens. I grip her hand even more tightly, pull and lift. Breezie does the same. With sudden ease we yank her from the precipice up to the surface. As soon as she stands up, she breaks into a broad grateful smile.

"Harlequins, you've just exhibited not only courage but the outmost compassion and caring for someone in peril, in this case me, overriding your own survival to first save yourselves. Congratulations, you've just successfully completed the last challenge thus, concluding your quest."

When she vanishes in a cloud of smoke, we are left standing at the exit of the tunnel wearing our harlequin clothes with the magnificent, Prague's Hradcany Castle appearing in front of us. We all jump for joy and celebration, hugging each other profusely.

The doors of the castle open in slow motion and we walk in, eager to be received and accepted. In the middle of the main hall stands the burly man —The Orloj— grinning broadly at us. On my shoulder sits Thumbpee and hovering around is Buggie!

"Follow me harlequins." The Orloj says with a thunderous voice.

As we walk the burly man human version of the clock swipes his hand in front of him. The spell he casts is incomprehensive. Instantaneously we are walking the halls of a different building. They are of elegant and cavernous baroque design.

"We are in a Jesuit University that dates back to the 16th century."

He walks with bouncy steps into a separate chamber. It is a magnificent two-story library with terracotta and dark wood tones. It has continuous vaulted ceilings with exquisite paintings in soft pastel colors matching the ornaments and furnishings. The ground floor has numerous mechanical earth globes lined in between the beautiful shelves containing countless precious antique books and manuscripts.

"This is the place I've chosen for your induction ceremony; it is called the Klementinum. Centuries ago, the famous astronomer Kepler, worked in here."

With our credentials as wizard apprentices on hand, we follow him outside. Then climb an adjacent tower after him. Once atop we can see Prague's city line filled with spires sparkling in the distance.

"Harlequins you've now become youngster wizard apprentices," he says, handing each of us our credentials. "For the next level of wizardry achievement, I'll be seeing you in the year to come during the same season, but in a different location. The wizards and witches' festival is also celebrated at the same time in a city inundated by water and seagulls."

As he vanishes, we are back to Staromestske Namesti (the old town city square). The six of us hug for what seems like not long enough. One by one we climb back onto the clock's scaffold. Once I enter inside, I am surprisingly alone, alongside the clock's mechanisms. Slowly my vision becomes blurry once more. In the distance as if frozen in time, I can see images of my parents and the antiquarian Mr. Kraus. Then, I am sitting with them, and as they pick-up where we left off, our conversation continues right there where we left it..., or perhaps just a tad forward.

"Young Erasmus, what is your reaction to what I've just read?" You seem to be drifting lost in thought somewhere else. Were you paying attention?" Mr. Kraus the Orloj antiquarian sternly questions me referring to the upside-down world scribble he earlier read.

"I loved it, Sir, every minute of it, especially the ending at Prague's castle," I reply, and Kraus is about to react but thinks better and simply just winks at me in recognition.

After thanking Mr. Kraus for everything, my parents and I part ways with the old antiquarian. Once more, I find myself in current day Prague walking the streets of the mysterious city. I glance ever so briefly at the sculpted gargoyles sitting on many roofs. I notice the countless spires that adorn the top of the buildings throughout the city, but this time none of them are moving.

When we walk past The Orloj, there is no scaffold present, but of course it is the middle of the day, and the parallel Prague is dormant for another year. Walking past the ancient clock, I feel a jolt of excitement when it seems, if just for a fraction of a second, that the dear gigantic clock as Mr. Kraus just did, also winks at me.

Chapter 10

"Epilogue"

**Erasmus and Victoria's Home
Boston (2030)**

For reasons never explained to me, we fly to Boston instead of Wales for a few days layover before we return to Hay-on-Wye. It is there, while sitting with my uncle Bartholomeous (who's also my stepbrother), who happens to be the only other person in the world that I would ever reveal my adventure to. Thanks to him I discover where I will travel to next year for my trials of wizardry apprenticeship.

"Erasmus, the place The Orloj referred to is Venice, Italy. The historic town is inundated by water, ancient books, and seagulls, specifically at its main square where a fabled historical clock sits. It bears the same name as the square. The St. Mark Clock, that's where you will be going next. I'll take you myself so you can also spend time with your Italian aunt and uncle. Their mother also happens to be an antiquarian as well," declares my uncle full of enthusiasm.

"The Central Valley Institute of Arts and Literature"
(2055)
Central Valley, California.

Erasmus Cromwell-Smith II returning out of his trance, brings his class back to the present. Even though commencing with this academic year, he aimed to make it an evocative affair, talking about his father —the eminent (R.I.P.) professor bearing the same name— but instead, evolved it into a deeply emotional journey through one of his childhood adventures.

"Next semester, I'll be taking you to Venice, Italy. The place of my second adventure."

"Awesome!" responds the class in unison.

In summation he refers to the fact that we all take for granted so many things that are actually privileges and deeds to be appreciated and enjoyed in life. Problem is that most of us don't recognize nor value them enough or simply not at all, until they are gone.

"Awesome!" Says the young professor. "See you all after the summer break. I wish you all a great time while on vacation, and now, you all go and FLY A KITE!"

Professor Cromwell-Smith II dismisses his class. Then leaves at a brisk pace. To everyone's astonishment, he pulls out of his sac a small kite and carries it on his shoulder as he leaves the auditorium.

The moment he exits, social media across the nation's dominions explodes. A new national obsession begins (again) directed at wizards and witches in the magic tale of The Orloj.

Acknowledgment:

Special thanks to D. Suster and Elisa Arraiz. Your invaluable help and blind faith on my work have been an intrinsically part of the creation of The Orloj. Also, Daniel Dorse for his masterful work on The Equilibrist series audio books. Thank you all.

About the Author
Erasmus Cromwell-Smith II is an American writer, playwright, and poet. The Orloj series has been crafted through a very intense and intimate introspective dive into the author's own life experiences and wisdom. Volume 2, The Orloj of Venice will be published in the Spring.

www.ingramcontent.com/pod-product-compliance
Lightning Source LLC
Chambersburg PA
CBHW030748110726

47900CB00008B/2508